Julian Halsby studied history and history of art at Emmanuel College, Cambridge, before embarking on a career of lecturing, writing, and art dealing. He lectured in London art colleges and ran a gallery in North London. Julian has written six books on art history as well as many articles on art criticism and is a member of The Critics Circle. He is also a painter, an elected member of the Royal Society of British Artists. Julian has lectured for The Arts Society for many years.

These stories were written between 1995 and 2021.

For Miranda.

Julian Halsby

# When Reason Dreams

Modern Ghost Stories

Austin Macauley Publishers™
London • Cambridge • New York • Sharjah

A CIP catalogue record for this title is available from the British Library.

ISBN 9781528940375 (Paperback)
ISBN 9781528941273 (Hardback)
ISBN 9781528941891 (ePub e-book)

www.austinmacauley.com

First Published 2023
Austin Macauley Publishers Ltd®
1 Canada Square
Canary Wharf
London
E14 5AA

# Table of Contents

# A Chancy Business

"Art dealing is a chancy business," Rupert Gilkes was wont to say. "There's a chance that you might find an exceptional picture; there's a chance that you might be able to buy it at a reasonable price; there's a chance that you might be able to sell it and there's just a chance that you might make a profit on the whole operation. People don't need pictures, so unlike the corner shop, my gallery can be empty for days. Then comes your chance, the big one!" Rupert would also admit, however, that dealing was a way of life he would not swap for anything else.

The Gilkes Gallery was well known in Hampstead, situated conveniently in Flask Walk in the centre of this urban village. Rupert had established the gallery in the early 1970s as a young man, having spent three delightful years reading history at Lincoln College Oxford followed by four rather more stressful years in the nineteenth century painting department of a major London auctioneer. Ambition was not one of Rupert's faults; he genuinely loved British art and was happy researching a minor artist or painting through old lists of exhibitors at the Royal Academy or Royal Society of British Artists. He was also at home in the sale room, especially the smaller rooms in London or the country where he could meet colleagues to discuss the market, the antics of the 'West End Boys' or the inevitable lack of good quality at the right price.

Another favourite rendezvous was the Chelsea Arts Club where he could spend long lunches with friends and, less often, potential clients. Rupert enjoyed the life of a dealer, rising at a civilised time of the morning, walking from his house in Belsize Park to the gallery via the cake shop to buy elevenses for himself and his secretary, reading the papers at leisure before examining the catalogues and trade papers which flooded through the door each week. Long periods of inactivity alternated with bouts of great energy when exhibitions were mounted and major sales made.

The gallery was housed in an old shop which Rupert had done little to modernise, apart from renovating the shop front in its original style and installing new lighting. Indeed, he had acquired good examples of Arts and Crafts to furnish the two floors to look as much like a nineteenth century private house as possible, and he had found some original Voysey wallpaper for the walls. The gallery was both charming and original with pictures hung three deep up the walls, unlike the new generation of white walled and oak floored picture shops with their sparse hanging which had all but replaced the faded gentility of older galleries.

Art dealing is about people and Rupert was very good with people. A tall man with a good head of dark brown hair unaided by artificial dyes, Rupert was now in his mid-fifties. His easy going habits and old fashioned manners made him an attractive boss as well as a popular personality of old Hampstead. Although there was not always enough for them to do, Rupert insisted on employing a secretary, always beautiful young women who enjoyed working with their charismatic boss. Indeed, his first secretary was now his wife and mother of two teenage daughters. His current secretary, Serena, had been with him for two years and was as attractive and educated as his previous employees. He treated them well, taking them with him on buying expeditions to the country, lunching them most days in local Hampstead restaurants or sometimes at Chelsea Art Club and treating them like part of his family. Some might have wished for a more intimate relationship but Rupert was totally faithful. He was also liked by the West End dealers to whom he posed no threat, and often would benefit from leads that they had no desire or time to follow up.

In addition to the sociability of the art world, Rupert found himself the centre of life in Hampstead. Local residents would pop in for a chat or glass of sherry before lunch or after work, while shopkeepers would often stop by in the gallery to shelter from the rain or cold and express outrage at the new level of rents or rates. He would enjoy talking to the older residents about their memories of artists who had lived in Hampstead before the war, such as Stanley Spencer, Rudolph Schwabe or Mark Gertler and he always remembered personal details about the elderly residents, such as birthdays or anniversaries, which he used to great effect. None of this, of course, made money but his same skills were used towards clients, many of whom considered the Gilkes Gallery to be amongst the most interesting in North London.

The reader might be forgiven for feeling a twinge of jealousy at Rupert's way of life with its apparent lack of stress and all the time in the world to savour personal relationships. However, there is no worldly paradise and every Garden of

Eden has its serpent. Rupert's very own serpent was his lack of ambition, his desire to see life continuing along the charming route that he had established, coupled with an indulgent and expensive lifestyle. The world however was changing and leaving Rupert behind.

Hampstead had attracted many younger professional people who found the newer galleries to their liking with their more aggressive marketing, their lavish private views, and their somewhat brash style of modern painting. To some the Gilkes Gallery was a feature of Flask Walk but was not a place to spend real money. The art on display was exquisite and charming but would not, in their opinion, fit into their concept of a contemporary interior. A more aggressive stance as a dealer would have been an advantage, with maybe a move into more 'progressive' styles such as Vorticism, Surrealism or post-war British Abstraction. Maybe more spectacular exhibitions with wider publicity and marketing would have raised the gallery's profile but Rupert felt that he had established his own way of dealing, which had served him well for 25 years and saw little need to change.

In the early 1970s, the rent of the gallery had been a tiny percentage of the turnover but constant rent reviews coupled with high business rates now meant that the fixed overheads, which included lighting and insurance, represented a significant and onerous monthly outgoing. Moreover, the rise in art prices, while boosting the turnover figures, required ever larger investment in stock which had to be financed by borrowings. Rupert hated all this aspect of the business and pushed such bills aside until the last moment. Out of sight and out of mind they were but their effect on his bank balance were clearly evident to his accountant and bank manager.

Rupert had got to know and like his bank manager had secured a loan of £50,000 repayable as and when deals were made, an unusual and flexible scheme. However, when the manager was replaced, the bank demanded regular repayments of capital in addition to interest.

Rupert had also borrowed money from his brother and father-in-law both of whom were beginning to ask about repayment. In addition, he had numerous debts outstanding with fellow dealers and smaller auction houses. He hated figures but a calculation made late one evening on the back of an envelope suggested that his debts approached £400,000 while his stock at cost was worth around half of that figure. There was, of course, the house in Belsize Park as an asset but over the years he had increased his mortgage as the value of the house increased in order to fund the business. Of course, a couple of good deals … but the recession had made such deals rarer and more difficult to conclude. His wife knew nothing of these problems and he was sure that some deal would soon 'turn up' to put everything right. The envelope was quickly consigned to the waste paper basket.

The week beginning 18th October started badly with a letter from the bank demanding the missed September capital repayment of £820 combined with the same amount for October. The quarterly rent of £8250, due on 26th September was also overdue, and a saleroom in Norwich was demanding £5280 immediately or else legal action would be taken. Rupert calculated that he would thus need £14,350 by the end of the week. The weekend trading had raised £3750 from the sale of two watercolours but he had allowed the customer, an old and loyal client of the gallery, up to four weeks to pay. The situation was beginning to look serious but the sun was shining and Hampstead was looking its autumnal best. As Rupert filed the letters into the bottom drawer of the desk, his secretary being in Italy for the week, Mrs Muriel Ridge entered the gallery.

Over the years, Mrs Ridge had wasted hours, in fact days of Rupert's time. Her conversation was lively and interesting, especially when she reminisced about Hampstead before the war and her extravagant hats and outfits provided the gallery with a touch of the exotic, particularly decorative and stylish at private views. Mrs Ridge had never bought anything at the gallery and had drunk considerable quantities of wine and champagne but Rupert had no regrets. She often talked about the pictures she owned but had never discussed them in detail. The widow of a successful West End fashion designer, she had herself worked in the art trade many years earlier both as a gallery assistant and later in an auctioneers in the country. An extraordinarily active lady, Mrs Ridge was probably well into her nineties but looked 15 years younger.

"What brings you in here so early Mrs Ridge?"

"A lovely October morning, Rupert; I've been for a walk on the Heath already. I always walk between eight and nine o'clock whatever the weather, come sun or storm."

"You're too energetic for me."

"A young man like you! Are you busy, Rupert, because if not, I would like you to see my pictures. I have to be honest with you," she said lowering her voice and looking around the gallery. "Is your assistant here today?"

"No she's on holiday all week."

"I have to be honest with you and tell you that I would quite like to raise a little money. Not for me, mark you but for my grandson who married last year and is hoping to buy a flat in Hampstead or nearby. That would be marvellous, you know Rupert. My son has lived in Scotland for 20 years and I rarely see him but his son might soon be my neighbour. I said I would make a contribution towards the flat, so I would like to sell a picture or two. Could you come and give me some advice? As you probably know, I was in the picture trade myself many years ago but I can't pretend to know what's going on nowadays."

"I would be delighted, Mrs Ridge, but I'm not sure that I would be able to buy anything. You know business is not that good."

"Well any advice you can give me. When can you come?"

"I suppose now is as good a time as any. I never have customers on a Monday morning."

Mrs Ridge lived a pretty cottage near Flask Walk, a cottage that in a country village would be considered a modest affair, but which in Hampstead would probably cost more than the village manor house. They went through a bower of climbing roses and up the cobbled front path and while Mrs Ridge fumbled in her handbag for the keys, Rupert admired the perfection of her cottage garden.

"I've done it again Rupert, I've locked the keys inside."

"Have the neighbours got a set?"

"The neighbours? They're never there, out at work from dawn to dusk. No we'll go around the back where I always leave the back door key under a flower pot. It's not the first time I've locked myself out, you know."

The collection of pictures was not bad. Some worthy Victorian watercolours, a nice little oil of Japan by Alfred Parsons, a couple of watercolours by George Charlton who had been a friend and neighbour and some etchings of Venice by Mortimer Menpes. Mrs Ridge's late husband had been a collector in a small way, but none of the work was particularly exciting. Mrs Ridge, however, was convinced of its merit and value.

"You see, Rupert, although I've been away from the trade for years, no decades, I still follow prices in the papers and I watch the Antique Roadshow, so I have some idea about present day values. For example, this little oil of Japan must be worth £5000 or more. I'm sure you could sell it for more."

"I doubt that, Mrs Ridge. I don't want to disappoint you, but what you see on the Antique Roadshow is not typical. Prices for this kind of work are not that high at present."

Mrs Ridge was not to be convinced, and took Rupert up a very old and twisting staircase to see the pictures upstairs. After looking at more of the same, including a cupboard full of unhung pictures which comprised some very poor Victorian copies of watercolours by Birket Foster, they went towards her bedroom.

"There is only one picture in my bedroom and I would never sell it. It's a painting by Lucien Pissarro which I bought in a small country gallery many years ago. My father knew the Pissarro family quite well and as a child I visited the Pissarro family house, so when I saw it, I knew exactly what it was. Come and see it."

It is the dream of every art or antiques dealer in the world to come across something so beautiful, so rare and so unappreciated that his heart is stopped for an instant. Rupert's heart stopped then began to beat faster than ever before, for at last he had found the Big One, the ultimate deal that would make him seriously rich. The picture hanging over the bed was quite large and presented in an elaborate carved and gilded frame. It depicted a street scene in a city, at dusk and under snow. It was full of horses and carriages and people in cloaks and hats going about their business. The sky was a pearly pink fading to cerulean blue and the snow reflected both the sky and the street lamps. It was an exquisite masterpiece but it was not by Lucien Pissarro but by his father, the French Impressionist Camille Pissarro, and it was in Rupert's view a superb example of his Paris city scenes. The canvas was clearly signed 'Pissarro' in the left hand bottom corner.

"Now, Rupert," Mrs Ridge was saying, "you're going to tell me that this is not worth £50,000 which I know Lucien Pissarro oils are worth. You're going to say that it would be difficult to sell. Well, I don't actually care because I'm never going to sell it. It reminds me of so much and it has always hung in my bedroom."

"No, it's lovely, it's worth every penny of £50,000. I'm not sure that it's by Lucien Pissarro ..."

"You art dealers, you always have to know better. I can tell you it's by Lucien Pissarro because it's signed on the back as well as the front."

With Rupert's help she took the picture off the wall and pointed to an inscription, now totally illegible, with the signature of Lucien Pissarro. To Rupert's eye this was probably a testimony by Lucien that this was the work of his father. Too stunned to say more, Rupert promised to investigate the possibility of selling some of Mrs Ridge's other pictures before seeing himself out of the house.

The image of the Pissarro painting haunted Rupert for the entire week, and he was unable to settle on anything else. The exquisite balance between natural light at dusk and the artificial light of the street lamps; the fine brushwork which encompassed people, horses, buildings and sky in an envelope of subtle atmosphere; the composition which balanced buildings, people and snow effects into a harmonious whole; all these remained in Rupert's mind.

Research quickly indicated that it was a painting of the Avenue de L'Opera in Paris and had never been listed or seen in a public exhibition while its value was probably somewhere over £8 million. Several plans began to take shape in his mind. Maybe he should offer Mrs Ridge £100,000 for the picture as a Lucien Pissarro, maybe that would tempt her to sell. He could then discover to his amazement and surprise that it was really a Camille. Maybe he should tell her the truth and admit that it is was a Camille and probably worth millions, and that he could sell it for maybe a 10% commission. Of course, there would be no guarantee that Mrs Ridge would not go directly to a top saleroom and cut him out.

Later that week Rupert Gilkes began to face the final reckoning. He received a letter from his bank stating that as he had failed to meet either the capital or interest payments on his loan for two months and as his current account was in unauthorised overdraft to the tune of £24,500, the bank was intending to call in the loan and take charge over the lease and assets of the gallery. He was given exactly five working days to propose a solution acceptable to the bank. During a series of restless and tortured sleepless nights he began to formulate a plan of action. Having ascertained that Mrs Ridge's son knew nothing about, and had no interest in, her pictures and that they were not listed for insurance purposes or probate, he decided to steal the Pissarro and attempt to sell it privately and discretely. This might not raise the full potential value of the picture, but it would more than cover all his debts and leave him several million pounds better off. To salve his conscience, he decided that he would anonymously pay Mrs Ridge the £50,000 she thought the picture to be worth, possibly by overpaying for one or two of her remaining pictures.

The plan was simplicity itself. He knew that Mrs Ridge was out walking every morning between 8 and 9 o'clock and that her neighbours were at work all day. He also knew where the back door key was kept so he could enter, create some chaos in the sitting room to suggest an ordinary burglary, and leave quickly with the picture. He would get up early, leave a note in the gallery for his secretary to say that he was attending a sale in Cambridge that morning and that he wanted to get there early to view it, and leave his car in a small street behind Mrs Ridge's cottage. Having removed the painting, he would drive out towards Cambridge, and somewhere around Royston would remove the fuse of his fuel injection system replacing it with one that had failed some time ago. He would then call the RAC who would keep a record their call out time thus providing an iron-cast alibi, in the very unlikely event that the finger of suspicion fell on him.

The plan went smoothly at first. Rupert waited in the car until he saw Mrs Ridge leave for the Heath, he quickly let himself into the house and went straight upstairs to remove the Pissarro. Then he heard the front door open and steps on the stairs; he came to the top of the stairs, the picture in his hand, and saw Mrs Ridge half way up.

"Rupert, you gave me a fright!" she exclaimed. "I've just come back for my gloves." She added rather illogically before demanding what he was doing in the house.

"I've just come to have another look at the Pissarro."

"No you haven't. You've come to steal it. I really didn't expect that of you, Rupert."

She advanced up the stairs and took hold of the picture by its frame.

"Not that one, Rupert, not that one. Take anything else if you must, but not that picture."

Rupert protested that he had no intention of stealing anything, but Mrs Ridge was tugging hard at the picture trying to wrench it out of his hands. He was surprised at her strength. Pulling hard at his side of the frame, Rupert managed to free the picture from her hands, but Mrs Ridge, no longer able to pitch her strength against his, lost her balance and fell backwards down the twisting staircase. She appeared to do a complete backward somersault, ending up on her back lying down the stairs, her head propped against the wall. Amazingly her extravagant black hat was still pinned to her hair, giving her tortured face an absurdly comical expression. A small trickle of blood ran from her mouth. In an instant Rupert knew she was dead.

His first reaction was total panic. Dropping the picture, he ran down the stairs stepping over the body as he went towards the back door. However, as he began to open it, panic was superseded by cool logic. He listened outside but there was no sound of neighbours raising the alarm; then he went to the front door, but apart from a few people going into the village with their baskets to shop, the road was quiet. Sitting down he began to run through his options, quickly deciding to continue with his plan. He had not had time to create havoc in the sitting room, so there was no evidence of his entry; moreover, apart from his finger prints on the frame and back door key, there was no evidence that Mrs Ridge had not simply fallen in her house, a sadly common occurrence amongst old people.

As he stood thinking in the front room he heard a series of loud bumps. Running to the bottom of the stairs, he saw that Mrs Ridge's body had slipped down the stairs, her legs now facing downwards, and her face staring straight at him, lifeless and white, but with a hideous grimace, still framed by the black hat which was now worn at an absurd angle. Stepping once again over the body, he went upstairs, filled the obvious gap on the bedroom wall with one of the poor copies of a Birket Foster watercolour which happened to be of a similar size, carefully wiping his finger prints off the glass. He then left the house, relocking the back door and replacing the key under the flower pot. He put the picture in the boot under a blanket and set off. The time was now just after a quarter past eight, and the whole operation had taken less than 20 minutes.

On the drive towards Cambridge, Rupert ran through the revised situation. He would stick to the original plan with the exception that he could now offer the picture through a major sale room rather than privately through a dealer, thus increasing his potential gain. He thought it prudent however to suggest that it should be sold abroad, possibly the United States just in case some relation of Mrs Ridge might recognise it. He also decided not to have the picture illustrated in the catalogue for the same reason. However, he considered the chances of someone recognising the painting as extremely slim.

"An extremely good example," said the head of Impressionist Paintings at Sotheby's a few days later.

"I'm really most impressed Rupert. We've had nothing as good as this by Pissarro for some years. We'll have to do some research on provenance and background though."

"Value?"

"Depends if we can arouse sufficient interest for some competitive bidding, but you must be looking at over £8 million, maybe £12 million on a good day. I suggest we keep it back until the spring when we can market it widely."

"No I'd prefer to sell it as soon as possible."

The director looked up momentarily. "Any reason?"

"Yes. Although I did a good deal, it stands me in at a fair amount and I would like a quick sale."

"It could just make New York for the November sale, but the catalogue is already out so there would be no illustration."

"Ideal. Let's go for it."

Armed with Sotheby's estimate, Rupert was able to hold his creditors at bay until mid-November when the sale took place in New York. The result was a triumph for Lot 173 Camille Pissarro 'Avenue de L'Opera, Evening Snow Effect'. Its provenance was unclear but there was a written message by the artist's son stating that the picture had been found in the artist's studio after his death. There was no question of the picture's authenticity and this, combined with its fine colours and atmosphere, led to competitive bidding between a private American collector and a Japanese company. The result was a sale to the American at $18 million, realising well over £11 million for Rupert after expenses. The sale result was faxed through to the gallery and Rupert began the celebrations by taking his secretary out to a champagne lunch in the West End having already faxed the sale result to his bank and secured a further extension of his overdraft. Knowing the extent of gossip in the art world, Rupert was careful not to advertise his success too widely. Several colleagues had heard that he had had a 'Big One' but none knew the exact details, and he was happy to keep them in their state of ignorance. This did not mean, however, that he should not celebrate, so he arranged a lavish Christmas party to be held at the Chelsea Arts Club to which he invited all his colleagues, which comprised a fair portion of the art world.

The residents of Hampstead had been shocked by Mrs Ridge's tragic death, and her funeral service at Christ Church was well attended. Amongst the congregation was Rupert Gilkes who had been temporarily shocked by a visit to the gallery by the police a few days after neighbours had found her body.

"I believe you were one of the last people to see her alive, sir."

"What do you mean by that?" Rupert had asked in some alarm before taking himself in control.

"I am led to believe that Mrs Ridge visited the gallery regularly and that …"

"Yes that's right. In fact, she was in last week, asking for a valuation of her pictures. I promised to come around."

"Did you visit her, sir."

"Er, no. We planned to do a valuation next week. I was rather busy at the time, you see."

"Yes, sir. Well, it seems that she didn't suffer too much. The pathologist suggested that she died shortly after her fall."

"Very sad; she was a real character and she'll be missed."

As the policeman was leaving, he turned to Rupert.

"One other thing, sir. I suppose Mrs Ridge never gave you a list of her pictures did she?"

"No, of course not," Rupert replied as calmly as he could. "Although I did suggest that we should make such a list for insurance purposes."

The party in their Hampstead house was an enormous success. The reason for the celebration, if one had been required, was 25 years of the Gilkes Gallery, although it was widely known that Rupert had scored a notable success in discovering an unknown masterpiece, the details of which remained obscure. Rupert and his wife were at the centre of a group of friends and colleagues and the party lasted well into the night. It was towards the end of the party that Rupert heard a knocking on the door behind him leading to the garden. He turned around and caught sight of an old lady gesticulating to him to open the door. He was surprised to see someone in the garden on a cold December night, but he went to open the door, but as he did so he saw the awful image of Mrs Ridge, her face white with pain, the trickle of blood still oozing from her mouth, her large black hat set at a comical angle. He tried to shut the door on her, but she had her foot wedged in the gap.

"You won't enjoy a penny of my picture! Not a penny!"

Suddenly the door flew open and a cold gust of wind swept across the room. The noise of party evaporated for a moment as everyone turned around in surprise.

"Trying to sober us up are you, old chap?" someone shouted as the noise of the party started up again.

Rupert's wife went over and locked the door. "I've never felt quite such a cold draft before; it seemed to blow right through me."

Rupert said nothing.

For weeks afterwards Rupert was haunted by the vision of Mrs Ridge, and, in his imagination, he began to see her everywhere. It was a very cold Christmas and New Year and many people were wearing hats, many similar to Mrs Ridge's exotic styles. In Hampstead High Street, on the Heath, even in the West End Rupert saw people he imagined to be Mrs Ridge, and at times he would run up to them and tap them on the shoulder, but much to his, and their embarrassment, they were strangers. And yet, he felt her presence everywhere. His sleep was disrupted and his appetite impaired, not a good thing over the festive season. But the real shock came early in January when Rupert phoned Sotheby's from the gallery to enquire about the likely date for the payment of his £11 million.

It was a very grey morning and flurries of snow swirled around the shop window. A few shoppers, well protected against the elements wandered up and down Flask Walk.

"I'm afraid, Rupert, that there is a little problem."

"What sort of problem?"

"Well, I'm not sure if it is serious at this stage, but I have to tell you that Prof. Rheinhart at the Barnes Foundation in Philadelphia is querying the provenance of the Pissarro."

"In what way?"

"It seems that a picture of the same subject and same size was stolen from a provincial saleroom in England in the 1950s. We can't be sure that this is the same picture, but we certainly cannot release any funds due to you at the moment. Can you tell us a little more about how you came across the painting?"

As he was about to reply, the gallery door opened and Mrs Ridge face appeared.

"I warned you not to take that picture, Rupert," she said with a loathsome smile.

"You stole it!" Rupert said dropping the phone and rushing towards the door.

"What sweet irony in that statement!" Mrs Ridge replied.

"You witch!" Rupert shouted reaching the door and grabbing the figure.

"Rupert! Have you gone mad?"

Serena, his assistant, stood at the door in her dark coat and hat extricating herself from her boss's hands.

"What's going on?"

Rupert sank into a chair by the door and buried his face in his hands. "What a mess! What a bloody awful, shitty mess!"

Rupert's worst fears were confirmed some days later when it was established beyond reasonable doubt that the Pissarro painting had indeed been stolen from a provincial auctioneer while waiting to be sent to London for expert valuation. The original owners were acquaintances of Lucien Pissarro and had bought the painting from the family. They had kept photographs and full documentation of the picture in the expectation that one day it would find its way back to the art market.

Worse still was the fact that somehow the story had got into the 'Daily Telegraph' along with a photograph of the painting and Mrs Ridge's son had recognised the picture as belonging to his mother and was now querying where it had gone. Within a few days, Rupert had received another, much less pleasant, visit from the police who had removed his passport and requested him to report back to the police for further questions. On Friday 18 January, the bank took possession of the gallery and its contents and the building society repossessed the Gilkes' house, Rupert's wife having gone to live with her parents taking the two girls with her.

Rupert still had the keys, and on Saturday morning he made a last visit to the almost empty gallery. The whole affair had been widely reported in the 'Ham and High', the local newspaper and although no mention had been made of the police's suspicion, it was common gossip that Rupert Gilkes had somehow stolen or removed a valuable painting from an elderly widow who had died shortly later. He saw old clients, friends and local shopkeepers passing by the shop without looking in. After some hours contemplating the bleakest of futures, Rupert went to the hardware shop to buy a length of rope. As he walked towards the Heath, he passed Mrs Ridge's cottage. She was in the front garden clearing the snow from the steps. He went to speak to her, but she held up a finger to her lips.

"Say nothing, Rupert. It's all over now."

Rupert Gilkes' body was found several days later hanging from a tree near the Vale of Health by a couple of women walking their dogs.

# A Stuart Tragedie

Dr Edwin Law was an unusual academic, being a 'doer' as well as a thinker. His subject was English Literature, more specifically Elizabethan and early Stuart, and more specifically still, the work of Ben Jonson on whom he had written the standard biography. But far from confining himself to critical analysis, Ed, as he was always known, was actively involved in directing, acting and promoting the many plays written in the late Elizabethan period, but quite overshadowed, both today and in their time, by the work of Shakespeare. As an undergraduate at Oxford, he had acted in a number of Shakespearean roles, and this had led him to explore the plays of Shakespeare's contemporaries, culminating in a production of Jonson's *Volpone* at the Bernard Sunley Theatre in St Catherine's College.

This highly acclaimed production, combined with an excellent first in English Literature, ensured a three-year doctoral fellowship at St Catherine's, and it was during this period that Ed began his work on Jonson. He continued to direct, and act in, a number of Jacobethan plays receiving enthusiastic reviews in both the national newspapers and literary reviews. In particular, he was praised for his careful analysis of the text and judicious editing which somehow breathed life and fire into his productions. He was now a Fellow of the college and a part-time lecturer in the English faculty, a post which allowed him the time to research and direct.

One of the most exciting aspects of Ed's research was the element of detective work involved. A considerable number of Jacobethan plays had been performed a few times before their manuscripts were consigned to oblivion. Most were lost, but occasionally original manuscripts did come to light in libraries, often wrongly attributed or misfiled. There was always an element of thrill in producing a play, however short or slight, that had last been performed in, say, 1598. Ed had one preoccupation in this field of literature which had exercised his mind for a number of years since starting his thesis on Jonson. He was convinced that Jonson had written a tragedy which, for some obscure reason, had been lost, or rather deliberately suppressed. There was very little evidence to support this theory, but just enough to keep the idea at the back of his mind.

Ben Jonson's life had been dramatic, violent and unpredictable. He had spent time in prison for the murder of a fellow actor, and in view of this chaotic lifestyle, it was likely that some of his work would have been lost. However, Ed had been fascinated by a sentence in a letter of 1609 written by a colleague of Jonson which referred to 'the kinge's grete displeasure at the tragedie of Stafford'. After completing a lecture at Birmingham University, Ed had driven up to Stafford to spend some fruitless time in the library studying the records from 1605 to 1610. He had been unable to find any connection between Jonson and Stafford either as a place or as a family. Why the king had been displeased was also a mystery, and of course, the word ‘tragedie’ could apply equally to an accident or death as to a work of literature. In another, quite unconnected, reference Ed had come across mention of ‘the Lord Compton’s grete anger’ and Ed could clearly envisage the trouble caused by this difficult, but brilliant playwright. And there, grounded in two contemporary errors, was the key to Edwin’s hunch.

It was several years later that, quite by accident, the two errors registered to form the first clue. Ed and his wife were keen walkers and would often drive out of Oxford on a Sunday to discover the countryside on foot. This they sometimes did by themselves or with a group of fellow enthusiasts. On this particular Sunday, the group drove north out of Oxford, through Woodstock and on to Kiddington where they left the cars. They then took footpaths to Steeple Barton and on to Compton Stafford. For a while, Ed could not work out why the village sounded familiar, then with a growing sense of excitement, he realised that it was possibly here, in a village with a historic manor house from the Elizabethan period and a Norman church, that the king had been so displeased with Mr Jonson.

The walkers admired the house from the outside until invited by the owner, who was cutting the grass, to stroll around the house and visit the church. The house was a good example of late Elizabethan stonework, well-proportioned but not too large, with some lovely carved details around the windows and doors. It had been built around 1570 following a fire which had destroyed the earlier fortified manor which had dated to the early fourteenth century. To the left of the house was a high wall, which the owner explained, had been part of the earlier building. It was attached to the rear wall of the house on one side, and to the east end of the small Norman church on the other, thus creating a sheltered and walled courtyard between house and church. The latter had originally been the manor's private chapel, the owner explained, but since the building of the new house around 1570, it had also served as the village church. After the group had moved on, Ed asked the owner, a London barrister, whether the Compton family still owned the manor. The reply was that, as far as they knew, there had never been a Compton family, the last aristocratic owners being the Varneys who had sold it in 1832. Ed explained his interest in the house and was invited to return at a suitable time to examine the books in the library.

A few days later, Ed returned to Compton Stafford where the housekeeper showed him to the library explaining that most of the books were modern except for three record books which had been placed on the table. These were fascinating accounts of the food and drink purchased and consumed by the household from 1577 to 1832 when the last Lord Varney had sold up. Also noted were sums paid to builders, lawyers, agents and merchants. The records were mostly written by the chamberlain, but with occasional notes added by the various Lord Varneys. It was with trembling hands that Edwin turned to the year 1609, and here after many years' speculation, was proof that King James had visited Compton Stafford and had seen a play by Jonson, or at least part of a play. The entries connected to the king's visit began in May when there were invoices for timber to be used in making 'a great stage for the players'. As the visit or 'progression' came closer, so the bills for food, wine, hay, material and labour grew in size and number. There was also a payment to 'Mr Jonson and his companie' written in Lord Varney's own hand. At the bottom of a page full of figures was a terse statement, again in Lord Varney's hand:

'Mr Jonson's tragedie was performed before the Kinge and many nobles. The companie was gretely disturbed and the Kinge did order the playe to stoppe. The Lord Varney had the playe encompassed in the world, where it might not be seene.'

The library offered up no further guidance as to what had actually happened and Ed remained puzzled by the fate of the play 'encompassed in the world where it might not be seene.' The first task was to research more into the life of the seventh Lord Varney and this was an easy task in the Oxford libraries. He had been born in 1563 and had worked for many years as a young man as secretary to Sir Robert Cecil in London. He returned to live in Compton Stafford on the death of his father in 1603 and served as judge in the Blenheim Assizes. He was interested in literature and the theatre and wrote a number of unpublished sonnets. The family had connections with Merton College which had received substantial endowments from the Varneys over many generations. Ed had not been aware of the connection between the Varneys and Merton College and his next visit was to the college's superb mediaeval library where he spent time going through books bequeathed by the Varneys and stamped with their arms, but despite finding some early editions of Ben Jonson, he found nothing which could throw more light onto the Compton Stafford mystery.

The trail appeared to have gone cold and Ed found himself pulled back into college and theatre work, but at nights he would lie in bed wondering what actually had happened on that day in June 1609. *Had the contents of the play offended the court on religious, political or even sexual grounds? Had*

*Jonson made play on the king's homosexuality?* Ed knew that Jonson was something of a royal favourite and that he had performed masques for the Queen and Prince Henry, and it seemed unlikely that he would have jeopardised his position with some ill-conceived scandal. He tried to visualise the small courtyard transformed into a theatre, but his mind constantly returned to the problem of what it had been that had so offended the king. He also spent time playing with the words 'encompassed in the world' but even with his knowledge of early seventeenth century English, he could make no sense of it.

On several occasions he returned to Merton College library and carefully noted every detail on the Varney bequests; books, church silver, donations to fellows, items of furniture including elaborately carved chairs for the Fellows' rooms and two magnificent globes donated to the library when the last Lord Varney sold up in 1832. Then one night while lying in bed constantly recycling the problem, he suddenly realised that his answer might lie in the globes. 'Encompassed in the world' could conceivably mean hidden in a globe. Lord Varney had commissioned the play and presumably, however displeasing to the king, he would not want to destroy it. Suddenly excited, Ed rang a colleague from the English department who was a fellow of Merton and arranged to meet him that morning in the library.

The two globes stood at either end of the library, one dating to the mid-sixteenth century, the other some hundred years later. His requests to open the Elizabethan globe were met with some scepticism by both his colleague and the librarian, but it was agreed that a conservator would be asked to give an opinion. Some months later, after much lobbying and paperwork, Ed stood in a studio at the Ruskin School of Art along with some Fellows from Merton and colleagues from his faculty. The conservator had removed the globe from its frame, decided that there was something inside and the moment of truth was about to dawn. Having carefully wired the two halves of the globe to prevent any distortion when separated, the conservator gently prized them apart. As he did so, the assembled group edged forward to see inside, and there, in a perfect state of conservation, lay a manuscript.

It was the find of the century; a rediscovered play written in Jonson's hand and dedicated to his patron, Lord Varney. The story made the national television news and photographs of Ed holding the manuscript appeared on the front page of many newspapers. A BBC crew arranged to film a 30-minute programme about the discovery of the play promising a follow-up when the play was staged. Ed was interviewed for a number of American magazines and for a period was considered something of a celebrity in Oxford. As a result of the publicity, it was some time before Ed had the opportunity to study the manuscript in detail and his first target was to make a complete transcription of the handwritten text onto his computer. Then he could analyse the text in detail and hopefully plan a production of the play, the first since June 1609.

The play was entitled *The Duke of Serafino* and was in essence an Elizabethan revenge but with maybe more insight and characterisation than many such dramas. The story started with the old Duke of Serafino, an imaginary Italian Duchy near Naples, who had two very different sons. The elder was weak, spendthrift and interested in young boys, although Jonson was both discreet and tactful in describing this aspect of his character. The younger son, by contrast, was brave, hardworking and popular. On the death of the old Duke, the elder son inherited the title and set about to discredit his brother and steal his substantial estates. This he did by engineering a conflict with the King of Naples and then accusing his brother of treason by siding with the enemy. He was banished, his estates sequestered and worst of all, the Duke married his brother's beautiful fiancée. The younger brother settled in Naples where he worked hard, gaining the confidence of the King of Naples and successfully leading the Neapolitan army into battle. Meanwhile in Serafino, the Duke was reviled and hated by his people. Finally, he was forced to pardon his brother and bring him back to help run the Duchy, but his intentions were evil and he planned to have him murdered.

The Duchess had fallen in love with her old fiancé, in fact she had never ceased to love him and described the torture of being married to the Duke. Jonson hints that their relationship is far from platonic and a sense of electric attraction between the two is conveyed in the language. The final scene showed the Duke contracting to have his brother killed with three 'condottieri' who were in fact supporters of his brother. They leave the palace, ostensibly to murder the younger brother, but really to tell him about the treachery. In the meantime, the Duke spends an evening of dalliance with a young boy, again tactfully handled by Jonson, while awaiting the murderers' return. They burst into the room, are disgusted by the 'stench of corruption' and brutally murder him, without the knowledge or approval of his brother. Jonson finishes the play by having the murderers banished to Naples, but one feels that they will soon be back. However, justice is seen to be done and with Papal dispensation, the new Duke marries his childhood love becoming the popular ruler of Serafino.

The manuscript was fascinating, full of changes in the text which illustrated how the playwright was developing the play as rehearsals progressed. The main problem was deciphering a difficult and often very messy seventeenth century hand, and Ed found himself spending hours laboriously transcribing the text. After several weeks virtually full-time on the project, Ed was obliged to start preparing a new lecture series on the work of Marlowe, and he carefully saved the transcript onto his hard drive as well as making an external drive back-up which he locked into his safe. These precautions had been the result of bitter experience. However, when, after some weeks working on the Marlowe lectures, Ed returned to the manuscript he discovered that for some reason which he could simply not make out, there was no text in the file. Cursing at his stupidity, he went to the safe to retrieve the back-up, but it too was blank. Edwin's life was busy and he hated incompetence, of which this was, he swore, a prime example.

Some weeks later, having repeated much of the original work, the transcript was finally finished and Ed was able to start making detailed notes prior to publication. Even then annoying delays took place, for example when the publishers mislaid the annotated text, and at high table Ed was beginning to make jokes about the play being jinxed and wishing he had never rediscovered it.

Before embarking upon the production of *The Duke of Serafino*, Ed circulated the transcript to six of his colleagues inviting them to an informal discussion after Sunday lunch at their house in the Woodstock Road. This was an important opportunity for Ed to gain a different perspective on the play which might influence his approach to its staging. In view of this, he taped the discussion.

"I should start by asking whether you think this is a good play or not. Was it worth rediscovering? Maybe you, Desmond as faculty professor should answer that one first."

"I would certainly describe it as good of its kind. It is a typical revenge drama but Jonson has created something with more depth. I particularly like the way he sympathises with the Duke for being unsuited to government and cast in the wrong role:

"Thrice cursed that I should be born to governance, not by choice, nor by wish, but by birth alone, no more. Yet my heart seeks tranquil fields, dalliance, Not affairs of state …"

"Jonson has created a man both evil and likable, or least understandable. I appreciated his predicament, even if I disapproved of his actions. In a way he is a more attractive character than Shakespeare's Claudius who plays a similar role. Jonson never condemns his 'unnatural passions', in fact he makes light of them. In a way, the less attractive character is the younger brother who never sins."

"No, he most definitely does sin. He has sex with his brother's wife. If that isn't a sin, what is?"

"True, but there are mitigating circumstances."

"As a mere historian, I should not perhaps comment on the literary values of the play, but I have discovered an interesting historical footnote. When Ed sent me the play, something rang a bell at the back of my mind, and I have subsequently worked out where the connection lies. In 1483 the newly ascended Lord Varney had his brother banished for treason, almost certainly on a false charge. The brother joined the court of Henry Tudor, then in France, and he returned with

Henry to Bosworth. Lord Varney had remained neutral, although he was certainly a supporter of Richard. Shortly after Bosworth, Varney was murdered, probably on the orders of his brother, but the new king turned a blind eye to the whole affair. Later, the new Lord Varney married his sister-in-law. So you see, Jonson's play is a clever adaption of Varney history, and must have been written with the help of Lord Varney."

"Absolutely. The dedication in the manuscript reads 'To My Lord Varney who hath described this noble plot'."

"I don't know about 'noble' but it certainly shows that Varney had a hand in the play and approved its contents. But we still haven't got to the real issue – what so greatly offended the king?"

"The reference to homosexuality?"

"Maybe, but as we've said Jonson is very discreet and only hints at the Duke's proclivities."

"That's the real mystery. After all, it's a comparatively straightforward, short play written on commission with the help and approval of Jonson's patron. There is nothing offensive either on a political or personal note, no glowing reference to the Tudors, no disparaging comments about Scotland or the Stuarts, nothing. I suspect we'll never know why the king and his court were so upset."

"Maybe the actors hammed it up a bit much."

"Okay, but surely not to the extent of having the play banned and incarcerated forever in a global prison, if I can call it that. I agree with Ed: I don't think we'll ever know exactly what caused this outrage."

Rehearsals began after Easter in St Catherine's with the intention of running five or six performances in the college theatre before a grand finale, a full staging of the play in the courtyard of Compton Stafford on or around 15 June, the date which Edwin believed was the anniversary of its first, and last, performance in 1609. This final performance was to be broadcast live from Compton Stafford on BBC 2, and, much to the delight of Merton College in whom the copyright resided, this film of the production had already been pre-sold in several countries. There was great interest from the academic world in Britain and the United States, and many rehearsals were attended by visiting academics. The media was also in evidence either photographing or filming the rehearsals. All this attention produced many unforeseen problems as well as putting unnecessary pressure on the actors, so Edwin was forced to limit the amount of outside interference.

Rehearsals were dogged by problems, some simply minor irritations, others of a graver nature. On several occasions during dress rehearsals the electricity cut out, for reasons which no one could discover, and just one week before the first performance, the leading lady, the Duchess of Serafino, played by a brilliant and very attractive second year English student, destined for the stage, was seriously injured in a hit-and-run accident by the Carfax Tower. Ed's bitter comments at high table was that it was not just the king who was 'gretely displeased'.

Finally, the play was ready for its run at Oxford, and Edwin, at the best of times a stern critic, was quietly pleased with the results. The characters of the duke and his younger brother had developed well, and both actors had projected themselves well creating clearly identifiable personalities.

The banished brother's heartache for his fiancée, now his reluctant sister-in-law was poignantly performed:

"That my fair Isabel,
Wrenched from the true bed of love by foul
And dastard envie, to live, nay exist,
For existence be not life, with a prince
Of ignoble mien and unnatural thoughts.
I weep at night, and sigh by day. My sweet,
My lovely Isabel …"

Isabel herself, played by an inexperienced understudy, had an irresistible vulnerability, of which the actress was well aware and which she developed over the six performances. Ed himself, true to the tradition of the actor-manager, played a minor part, the King of Naples.

At the end of the run, the simple scenery and unpretentious seventeenth century costumes were packed up and transported to Compton Stafford where the stage in the courtyard was being erected. Over the months, Ed had returned regularly to the house to measure the courtyard and take in details of points of exit and entrance. The back of the stage was made up of the old wall which had formed part of the original fortified manor that had burnt down in 1570. It was a solidly constructed wall, built in local stone, and pierced at ground level by two doors which led to the garden behind.

On the higher level there were clear indications of three gothic windows which had been filled in with stone. The stage was constructed below the original floor level clearly revealing the stone corbels and holes for the main beams. On the wall behind were the remains of a fireplace with a small door, long since blocked up, next to it, and Ed had been careful to incorporate both windows and fireplace into his stage design.

Two portable cabins were installed behind the wall where the actors could change and await their entry, which was easily achieved by walking through the ground floor doors and up the steps constructed on either side of the stage. To the right was the side wall of the Elizabethan manor house, on which the lighting rigs had been hung, while to the left was the wall of the Norman church. The stage was about 45 feet wide and the acoustics were surprisingly good. Ed was delighted with the arrangement, and welcomed the BBC crew who were filming a programme about the preparation for the production. In an interview, Ed stressed the fact that the stage in June 1609 would probably have been very similar, maybe not quite so high, and that the king and his court would have sat in exactly the same place as the modern audience. Sadly, while the crew were filming the preparations; an electrician fell from the lighting rig, breaking both legs and his pelvis; worse still, the fall was recorded on camera during a live lunchtime news item.

The forecast on the morning of 15 June was mercifully good: Light clouds would disperse during the afternoon to leave a clear sky for the evening with just an outside chance of summer storms which would be unlikely to produce rain. The specially invited audience included many Oxford Fellows as well as business and publishing personalities many of whom had financially supported the venture. The audience numbered some 300, and as the play was quite short, a marquee had been set up in the grounds to provide an elaborate pre-performance buffet.

As the daylight faded, the TV lights came on, the courtyard taking a golden hue from the stone walls on three sides. Ed, dressed as the King of Naples, came onstage to make a very brief announcement, mainly for the benefit of the television audiences, in which he stressed that King James the First had sat in this very courtyard in June 1609 to see this very play. He explained the mystery of the king's displeasure and invited the learned audience to spot the politically or sexually offensive material. Then the play began.

There was little doubt in Edwin's mind that this was the best performance so far. The setting was exquisite: The honey coloured stone walls richly patinated with age, the clear azure sky with stars just beginning to reveal themselves and the gentle sounds of the Oxfordshire countryside, all made for perfection. The sense of occasion, the superb acoustics, the intimacy of the stage, the appreciation of the audience, all made for ideal circumstances and the actors rose brilliantly to the occasion. The treachery of the Duke in banishing his brother and stealing his fiancée came over darkly, as did the fate of the poor Isabel, abandoned and forced into a loveless marriage. The younger brother's nobility and bravery stood in stark contrast to the Duke's weakness and sloth; and yet the audience could sympathise with his predicament.

Then came the moment of the brother's return, forced upon the reluctant Duke by popular appeal, and providing an opportunity to rid himself finally of the major irritation of his life. Jonson had created an interesting stage play in which two events took place on either side of the stage, as if in two separate rooms within the palace. To the right, Isabel is reunited with her fiancé after years of separation:

"Sweet love, divine harmony

To live as one for evermore ..."

While to the left, the Duke is closeted with the three professional assassins planning to kill his brother. Jonson brilliantly contrasted the two scenes, creating a sense of evil foreboding.

What happened at this moment is still not clear. Some members of the audience believed that two figures had appeared at the front of the stage, others that they had actually walked through the door in the back wall by the fireplace. The young actress playing Isabel was immediately aware of two unknown people on the stage and with a mixture of anger and fear, stepped aside. Ed was off stage and only became aware that something was wrong when Jonson's dialogue stopped. Running around to the front to join the audience he shared their extraordinary vision.

The two people, a young woman of Isabel's age, and a young man, dressed in the elaborate night clothes of the mediaeval period were embracing on the stage. In place of the sparse stage scenery, a richer and more elaborate setting had emerged with an elaborately damasked room complete with Gothic chests and a four-poster bed. Their love was passionate and unfettered; they were obviously hungry for each other. At first many of the audience thought this was part of the play, and there was even a cat call from an advertising executive who had drunk too much champagne. However, as the act of carnal passion developed, the audience became restive and uncomfortable.

The younger man ripped off his heavy gown and nightshirt and stood facing the girl, his sexual arousal clear to all, while the girl slowly and languidly undressed revealing an exquisite white body. Then they consummated their passion on the stage, at times standing, at times lying on the bed, quite unaware of the audience. His passion was sometimes violent and the girl called out in mute pain, but no sound could be heard, the very silence of actors and audience imparting a strange eeriness to the scene. The audience gazed on transfixed by the extraordinary passion and energy of the couple who were quite oblivious to the outside world, and the spell of total silence was only broken by the wife of a college principal who declared the scene 'disgusting', but most of the audience sat transfixed with the unworldly vision.

Then, unseen to the lovers, but becoming increasingly clear to the audience, the shadowy figures of an older man, heavily built and attired in a fur gown and velvet cap, and three younger men armed with swords, emerged from the wall to the left of the stage. They appeared to be in deep conspiratorial conversation, before the three armed men departed through the wall. The audience was just aware of another figure seated at the front of the stage, a youth with blond hair. The older man approached the youth, kissed him gently on the lips and began to caress his chest. To the right of the stage, through a wall and unseen to the older man, the passionate couple continued their love making, while to the left, in a small and sparsely furnished garret, the boy disrobed his lover and they too indulged in passionate sex. For some of the audience this was too much, and several people began to protest; the majority remained mute, wondering where the acting had stopped and reality taken over. Time itself seemed to stop, and nobody could later say exactly how long the 'scene' had lasted.

The threat of a summer storm was slowly materialising, and a fresh wind was beginning to shake the leaves of the tall chestnut trees behind the stage. A sudden flash of lightening illuminated the stage just as the three armed soldiers returned. They appeared to knock at a door, before bursting into the scene of homosexual love. The older man was violently dragged away from his lover, the soldiers silently laughing at his arousal. Then in an act of total barbarism, one of the soldiers severed the man's member. A gusher of blood spurted over the youth who ran towards the front of the stage clawing at a closed window. As the first soldier laughed at the mutilated man's agony, the second thrust his sword up the boy's anus. His arms outstretched, his face contorted with pain, his body covered with his lover's blood which was mingling with his own, the boy slowly slid to the floor, leaving a trail of blood on the window. The three soldiers then turned their attention to the older man, poking his chest with their swords until they drew blood, slicing off his nose and genitals and hurling them towards the boy; all this while the lovers in the next room reached a further climax.

The reaction of the audience to the violence was varied; the eerie spell of silence had been broken by hoarse shouts of disgust and horror. Most of the audience were on their feet, while the film crew from the BBC were desperately explaining to London why they had blacked out the broadcast. Meanwhile on stage the final horrors were being enacted, as the soldiers repeatedly ran their swords through both bodies before opening the window and throwing out the hideously mutilated corpses. Then and then only, did calm slowly return. The soldiers disappeared through back wall; the lovers, one moment so real and carnal, slowly became ethereal and insubstantial; the window, stained and bloody, simply ceased to be there; the walls and furniture dissolved into air.

What seemed particularly strange was that this bloodthirsty scene, which appeared to have taken place over a period of some time, had actually happened within a few minutes. A great silence, the result of a mixture of physical exhaustion and relief, descended and it was some time before Edwin mounted the stage. There was no evidence of blood, no sign of discarded clothing, an empty stage awaiting the actors. But no actor would mount the steps, and no member of the audience wanted the play to continue. Some accused Ed of scandalous behaviour and outrageous cheek, but most realised that they had witnessed something quite out of human control. Few people spoke as they made their way back to the car park, shocked and confused.

The following day, Edwin gathered his college colleagues together to discuss the supernatural events at Compton Stafford.

"The Varney ghosts were just as shocking to us as they had been to James the First and his court. No wonder the king was 'gretely displeased', he must have thought at first that the actors were making fun of him. I think we all witnessed what James' Court had seen on that night in 1609, impossible as it might seem to us today."

"At least the Stuarts were superstitious and believed in spirits. I don't know what the press will make of the evening's fiasco, and even if they believe that they have witnessed a supernatural event, they would never admit it publicly. The extraordinary thing is that none of the vision was captured on film. Apparently in the broadcast the stage just empties and remains empty."

"Just as well," replied a colleague. "I wonder whether 'The Duke of Serafino' will ever be performed again?"

"Oh I'm sure, but never at Compton Stafford."

# Dawson

The house was perfect, just what Robert and Beth had in mind for their retirement. A fine stone house dating from the late seventeenth century with mullioned windows, a superb and quite grand oak staircase, well-sized reception rooms with good ceiling height, five bedrooms on the first floor and a substantial garden to one side. Since retirement, Robert had spent hours on the internet looking for suitable houses in the South West, but not too far from London where they still had many friends. They had made several visits to potential houses, but none quite matched the appeal of May Tree House. It was situated in Nether Sydling a village about eight miles south of Sherborne in one of the most beautiful areas of Dorset. The village itself was perfect with a couple of shops, a good pub and a beautiful church which dated back to the thirteenth century. Robert was a keen walker and appreciated the fact that Nether Sydling was considered a natural centre for hikers with a series of well-marked footpaths. The village nestled under steep hills on both sides protecting it against the worst of the winter weather.

They had both been captivated by the house on their first visit with the estate agent who showed them around before taking them into the slightly overgrown garden which lay on the East side of the house with a tall stonewall dividing it from a public footpath that led down past their garage and onto the start of a marked walk up the hill.

"The owners have moved into retirement accommodation and the house has been taken over by their son who lives in Manchester. He and his wife had hoped to keep it on as a summer house but the journey proved too long. They have spent very little time here and have decided to sell. This explains the rather unkempt garden, but I am sure you can soon restore it to its former glory."

"In your information pack you talk about a garden 250 feet long, but this is nowhere like that." Robert observed.

"To be honest, I don't know the property well. You are the first couple to visit and I didn't write the details. Let's see if there is more land at the back."

They walked down towards the stone wall at the bottom of the garden which was overgrown with honeysuckle and wisteria and spotted a door in the middle. Opening the door, they saw a huge second space which was totally overgrown.

"There's your answer," said the agent. "This must be over 150 feet long and goes right down to that wall with the ruined greenhouse. A wonderful restoration project for someone."

"A lot of hard work," said Robert, "but a real challenge."

"Two walled gardens!" added Beth. "Is that another door over there?"

"That leads out to the public footpath and the access to the garage. There are some superb walks on your doorstep."

Robert and Beth put in an offer at the asking price which was quickly accepted and started planning their move from London. Despite the state of the gardens, the house itself was in good condition with modern wiring, plumbing and a relatively new kitchen. They were able to move in once the legalities had been settled. Robert's immediate task was to clear the upper garden, as they called it, leaving the lower garden to the following season. He enjoyed working in the open air, so different from the years spent in a solicitor's office in the City of London. But sadly the enjoyment of his retirement was marred by a growing anxiety about Beth.

For some time, Beth had been complaining of stomach aches and pain after eating. A naturally shy person, she rarely spoke about it and certainly did not want to see a doctor unknown to her in a new location. Robert persuaded her to make an appointment with the woman doctor in London whom she had known for decades, only to discover that she had retired. She brushed off Robert's worries saying that she was suffering from indigestion, but she was often tired and the enjoyment seemed to have gone out of her life. Finally, in great pain she was persuaded to see a local doctor who quickly referred her to the County Hospital in Dorchester. The diagnosis was not good – cancer of the bowel which had spread to her stomach.

Beth took the news very badly, angry that destiny had robbed her of even a few years of happy retirement. She was not resigned to the likely outcome and vented her anger and disappointment on Robert. The consultant recommended a course of chemotherapy which made her both ill and depressed. After a series of long and very disturbing conversations with Beth, Robert decided that he needed a distraction from his domestic problems and that he would tackle the lower garden which they had completely ignored while getting the upper garden into shape.

He began pruning the wisteria and honeysuckle on the wall and cleared the area around the door which led into the wilderness, as they sometimes called it. For several weeks he worked hard, clearing brambles, elder bushes, dog roses, bind weed and nettles. Going through the doorway into the public footpath, he was able to load his car directly from the garden which made life easier and then drive to the municipal dump. He discovered the remains of a brick well and a rather unusual cast iron bench, but progress was slow and he still had a long way to go.

One afternoon when Beth had gone to bed Robert went into the garden to continue his work. He felt depressed and began to wonder why he was spending his energy on the project when he would probably have to leave May Tree House. Because of Beth's illness they had not been able to make the sort of friendships they hoped. They had not been able to join the bridge club and Beth could not sing with the local choir. Robert felt lonely and washed up in a place where he knew so few people. He began to feel that it would have been better to stay in London.

Then he smelt the rich aroma of a dark tobacco and assumed that someone smoking a pipe had walked down the passageway by the wall. He turned to look and saw a man sitting on the Victorian bench by the well he had uncovered smoking a pipe. He was a dressed in dark trousers, a blue smock and leather walking boots.

"This is a private garden," Robert said. "How did you get in? The gate to the footpath is locked."

The man did not reply to the question but continued smoking.

"This is the most beautiful garden in Nether Sydling, you know. Or it was, before it became neglected and overgrown. You should clear the greenhouse over there: It was the pride and joy of the Maitlands. They grew exotic fruit like oranges and pineapples there and it even had its own heating system."

The man stood up and walked towards the door.

"Good luck with your work," he said as he disappeared through the door to the footpath.

Robert went over to bolt the door but found it already bolted. Over the next few weeks Robert had little time to think about this encounter. He was committed to drive Beth to hospital for treatment and spent long hours trying to keep her optimistic and cheerful. He did find time to clear the way towards the greenhouse which was a fine example of a mid-nineteenth century wood and glass structure built directly against the end wall. Much of the glass was broken and the wood rotten, but Robert believed that it could be restored. He found the remains of a coal boiler which would have fed the hot water pipes some of which could still be seen beneath the tiled floor.

One afternoon he was working on the wooden window frames when he again smelt the rich aroma of pipe tobacco. He turned expecting to see his visitor again, and indeed he was standing by the door.

"This used to be one long garden before the Maitlands bought it," he said.

"Who are the Maitlands?"

"General Maitland bought the house when he returned from the Peninsular Wars and they stayed here for some 30 years. Lady Maitland did not like seeing the vegetable garden from the house, so she had the dividing wall built. She also had the greenhouse built and was a very enthusiastic gardener. She learnt about exotic fruits and flowers and her greenhouse was a wonderful sight." The man knocked the ash out of his pipe and slowly began refilling it. "Did you know that she changed the name of the house? It used to be called Battle House, probably because it was believed that there had been a battle here during the Civil War, which I very much doubt. Lady Maitland didn't like the name so she changed it to May Tree House. The may tree is still in the garden."

"You know a lot about this house. It's fascinating to hear all this. But I don't even know your name."

"Dawson."

"Mr Dawson?"

"Just Dawson."

Robert continued working on the wooden frame and soon realised that he was alone. Once again he checked the garden door, but found it locked. He began to suspect that Dawson might be a figment of his imagination, but in his depressed and worried mood he found comfort in their chats about the house. In bed at night he wondered about Dawson. *How old was he? Where did he live?* His accent was soft with a very slight West Country burr, but he was obviously an educated man, but he seemed ageless and very much part of May Tree House.

A few weeks later Dawson again appeared while Robert was working digging out elder saplings and bushes which had taken over the area in front of the greenhouse.

"There used to be wonderful cutting flowers there which Lady Maitland took into the house," he said drawing on his pipe. "She was a remarkable lady."

"What happened to her?"

"After her husband's death she lived on in the house for years, but always kept it band-box. She had help in the garden and the house, mind you. She continued to work in the garden until her dying day and she was well into her nineties when she died. She always said that it was the garden that kept her happy despite living alone. When she died the house was sold because her children had their own properties. The house changed hands quite a few times after that, but the garden was never as beautiful as when Lady Maitland looked after it. The younger son of a local farmer bought it in the 1880s and used the garden as a small holding. He grew vegetables in both gardens and fruit in the greenhouse, so it was well used."

Dawson drew deeply on his pipe and remained silent for some minutes.

"I like continuity, I don't like change."

Beth finally succumbed to her illness and Robert was distraught but had little time for sorrow. He had to arrange the funeral, contact his son who lived with his family in Australia, tell their London friends, and deal with all the legalities of death. The funeral itself in the church was sparsely attended because neither Beth nor Robert had had the time or opportunity to integrate into village life. Some friends from London and their son from Australia attended, but it was a sad and desolate funeral.

After the funeral and the wake when the guests had left, Robert sought solace in the lower garden. He found relief in the undemanding task of sanding the Victorian bench prior to repainting it. Even before he smelt the tobacco, he heard the comforting voice of Dawson.

"Churches are places where you find extreme joy and extreme sorrow. I've seen both, you know. I remember a day in May 1914 when Reg Hammond married Mathilda Webb. That was a wonderful day, the happiest event ever in the village. Reg was a lovely man, the son of the shopkeeper."

"Hammonds still exist."

"Yes, but it was Reg's brother who took it over. Now it's just a shop, but in those days it was a big business. The Hammonds ran the shop but also had a barn to sell agricultural produce, livestock feed, grain, fertiliser that sort of thing. They also introduced the first steam engines to the village. The Hammonds were rich, popular and very good for the village. Reg was over 6 feet tall and extremely handsome, yet despite his money and looks, he was charming, polite and friendly. Mathilda was the prettiest girl I've ever seen. Long dark hair, beautiful eyes, a wonderful smile. Everyone loved her and her wedding with Reg was a fairy tale marriage. I don't think the church had ever seen such a beautiful couple."

"After the marriage the Hammonds invited everyone to a party in the village hall. It was a warm May afternoon, the cherry blossom was out and spring flowers abounded in the fields. Everyone had a wonderful time. It was as if paradise had come to the village. Reg and Mathilda moved into May Tree House after their marriage, but their wedded bliss didn't last long. In August the war broke out and Reg signed up. He came back to the house a few times while he was training in Dorchester, but then he was posted overseas. The next we knew was that he had died at Ypres but his body had not been recovered. The church which had witnessed such joy in May, now saw deep sadness. Mathilda, the widow, was a frightening and terrible sight dressed entirely in black her eyes red from weeping. The whole village turned out for the memorial service and everyone was haunted by that happy day in May just six months earlier."

"What happened to Mathilda? Did she stay in the house?"

"She stayed for the war, growing vegetables, keeping rabbits and hens. She was a country girl who knew the country ways. After the war she married a landowner in Hampshire and moved on. However, she came back to Nether Sydling to baptise her children, so the church again saw joy and a future."

"I find it difficult to see any joy or future for me."

"You will find both. Why don't you join me for a drink at The Mitre? Have you ever been in?"

"When Beth was still walking we sometimes had a quick drink there after a ramble, but I haven't been in since her illness started."

"You need some friends and there's a pleasant group of drinkers there at the weekend, locals and weekenders. Join me there on Saturday, say six o'clock, for a drink. I'll wait for you in the bar."

Robert would not normally have gone into the pub by himself, but encouraged by Dawson he went down for a drink. Entering the bar, he saw Dawson seated at a table by the window. Going over to him he offered to buy him a drink.

"Mine's a mild and bitter."

Robert went to the bar to order the drinks and started chatting to a man seated at the bar.

"We were very sorry to hear about your wife, but you both seemed such a self-sufficient couple that we didn't want to interfere."

"It has been a very hard time, but I've now got to decide where I go from here."

The drinks arrived and Robert took them over to the table, but Dawson had gone. Assuming that he had gone to the lavatory, Robert sat down to wait for him. But after ten minutes there was still no sign of Dawson. Robert went back to the bar to ask if anyone had seen Dawson, to which there was no reply.

"Why don't you join me?" asked the man at the bar. "I'm Michael Seaton and I live opposite Hammonds in Ivy House." They were soon talking about their past careers, their love of walking in the hills, children and grandchildren and later Michael invited Robert around for a simple kitchen supper to meet his wife.

Over the next months, Robert found himself sucked into all sorts of local activities including a bridge club, a literary group, while his legal knowledge was put to good use in a Citizens Advice Bureau. He occasionally met Dawson in the lower garden while he was planting new plants, trees and bushes to replace the wilderness he had cleared, but his visits were less regular. Robert had considered finding out more about Dawson, where he lived and what he had been, but in heart of hearts he knew that Dawson was not of the world of the 'quick and living'. On the one hand Robert was embarrassed to ask his new friends about this unusual visitor, but at the same time he maybe did not want to destroy the relationship with a dose of reality.

Several months later, Robert was invited to a literary lunch in Sherborne where he met an attractive and interesting widow whose career had been in publishing. They 'clicked' and found each other's company interesting and stimulating. Robert took pride in showing her the two gardens especially the lower garden which he had restored with such determination and hard work. Laura was particularly entranced by the Victorian greenhouse which was now fully glazed and had its own heating system. There were courgettes, strawberries, raspberries growing and a vine was creeping up the back wall.

Their relationship developed over the following months, and one evening Laura came to dinner. It seemed natural to both that she should stay the night. Early the following morning Robert left Laura sleeping and took a walk in the garden. The familiar aroma of strong pipe tobacco drifted across the garden, and without looking around Robert said, "Hello Dawson. I haven't seen you for some time."

"Oh, I think I've told you everything you need to know about May Tree House."

"And that there can be joy after deep sorrow."

"Indeed. I'll say goodbye then. And don't worry, I'll lock the door after me."

# Friends for Life

"I was just 14 when we first visited Southwold in Suffolk in 1936. I remember that it was 1936 because there was all the fuss about the Spanish Civil War. I was a Londoner born and bred and I had hardly even seen the sea, let alone swim in it or play on the beach. I don't know why my parents decided on Southwold for that summer holiday except that my aunt, that is my mother's sister, had said that it was very 'nice'. It certainly was nice. I loved it on first sight; all those miles of beach, stony in front of the town itself, but sandy further up the coast."

I remember arriving on a brilliantly sunny day, and those white buildings just took my breath away. There's something about seaside towns; you always can tell that you're near the sea because the buildings shine in a way you never find in London. Brighton's like that, but Southwold is smaller and a better place for a lad of 14. I just wanted to get down onto that beach, but my parents made me help them unpack and do some shopping first. We had rented a pretty little house opposite the lighthouse with a view of the sea from the upstairs room. It's funny, I can remember that house quite clearly as though I had seen it yesterday. It didn't have a front door; well, that's not true, it did, but it was always locked, so you had to go up the side passage and through the back door which led into the kitchen. There were two bedrooms upstairs, a big one with the view of the sea, and a small one at the back where I slept. Downstairs, there was just one large room.

I was so excited that first day! Today we all take holidays for granted but in those days you rarely got a proper holiday, usually just a day in Brighton or somewhere. I suppose my father's business was doing better so we had a bit more money. He had a fruit and vegetable business in Covent Garden and always had to get up in the middle of the night. Anyway after we had unpacked we went down to the sea to rent a beach hut for the two weeks. That was lovely, a little house, nicely fitted out with furniture, just by the sea. I wanted to sleep there at night but my mother wouldn't hear of it. Sometimes I used to pretend that I was asleep at night in the hut listening to the roar of the waves on the stones. My mother was very protective, I suppose because I was an only child. I often wish that I had had a brother, then we might have been able to sleep in the hut. My mother did make a terrible fuss of me, always checking my clothes and seeing where I was. I was a bit of a loner, a quiet lad; self-contained is the word, I think.

That first morning, I can tell you, I was up with the larks. I slipped out of the house while Mum and Dad were still sleeping and went down to the sea. I suppose I must have been standing there for a good half an hour, just looking. Then I went back for Mum's cooked breakfast, and didn't it taste good. Something about the seaside, everything always tastes, and smells, better than in town. After that we strolled down to the harbour, not really a harbour more like a creek, but Dad managed to book us on a boat that was going out for an hour's pleasure trip. Out we went into the swell, and I felt frightened and excited at the same time. I think Mum was scared stiff: She just sat there looking straight ahead. I'll never forget that feeling of sun shining off the water like a mirror and that marvellous smell of the sea. I've smelt it many times since, but never with such intensity as on that first morning. Out we went and we looked back at Southwold with the long beaches stretching both ways. I would soon get to know those beaches really well, but on that morning I wanted to start exploring as soon as possible. We could just make out our house by the lighthouse and Dad told us about the lost village of Dunwich, which made me feel quite eerie.

We had a picnic lunch in the beach hut then I was finally allowed to explore. At first Mum wanted me to stay in sight, but Dad said that I could come to no harm, so, having been told to keep away from the big waves which could knock me off my feet, and not to talk to strangers, I was allowed to go. I heard Dad telling Mum about letting me grow up. Anyway I was off as fast as I could run with my bucket and spade, up the beach towards the sandy bit I had seen from the boat. It was here that I met them, the Stebbings boys; Albert and Thomas, always called Bertie and Tommy. They were making sandcastles near the sea and running into the big waves as they broke. I stood for a while watching them, too shy to speak, and then I started making my own sandcastle nearby. For a while they took no notice of me, although I kept on looking at them enviously.

I suppose I was envious of their companionship and sense of fun: Having no brother or sister, I missed all that. Then the elder one, Bertie, came over and said.

"That's a silly place to build a sandcastle."

"Why?" I replied.

"Cos the tide's coming in."

I wasn't sure what he meant, but I pretended to take no notice. Then with a laugh he jumped right onto the sandcastle scattering it around. I pretended to be angry and chased him towards the sea. He ran into a large breaker, and called for me to join him.

"I can't," I replied standing in a few inches of water.

"Why not?"

"Well, I'm not allowed."

"Not allowed into the sea? Don't be silly! Come on."

So in I ran and we were joined by his brother. We chased around, up the beach towards the clay cliffs, along the water's edge and into the waves. Finally, we collapsed onto the sand and introduced ourselves in that strange way that young children do. They asked me my name, and I replied "William."

"Billy!" They both shouted.

"No my mother hates that. I'm called William."

"Well we're going to call you Billy."

Bertie and his younger brother Tommy were both handsome lads, one 14 the other nearly 12. They looked very similar with sandy hair, ruddy complexions and faces covered in freckles. Both had tanned bodies which had been exposed to the sun and sea all summer, and compared to my white London skin, they looked very exotic, or so I thought. We didn't worry about skin cancer in those days. Anyway we got talking and I explained that I was on holiday in Southwold, and they told me that they lived there and that their father had a boatyard by the harbour and owned his own fishing boat. We talked and talked, then I said I better be getting back. So we all walked back to the stony beach and past our beach hut. I wanted them to meet my parents, but they said they better push on, so I waved to them from the hut. My mother asked who I was waving to, and I told her that I had made some new friends.

That I night, I tossed and turned in bed thinking about my friends and hoping the new day would come quickly. The next morning I was up first, wondering how I would meet Bertie and Tommy. Dad said that we should walk to Walberswick before it got too hot, so we went along to the harbour and took the ferry across. The ferry was a heavy rowing boat which an old boatman rowed slowly across the creek. As we got to the other side, I saw Bertie and Tommy standing on the jetty we had just left. I waved to them and they replied and shouted that we would play together in the afternoon. My father asked me who I was shouting to, and I told him about my friends. He looked across the creek and said that he couldn't see anyone, and that he must get some new spectacles.

We had a good walk in Walberswick and my father bought drinks in the old inn there. Mum said that he was really beginning to relax. After picnic lunch in the beach hut, I waited for my friends. I saw them beckoning to me and I was off. This time we went back to the harbour and sat inside a fisherman's hut that they knew was unoccupied. We talked and talked and played hide-and-seek running between the huts and boatyards. They showed me their father's yard and I saw men building a fishing boat inside. Creeping in, I smelt the marvellous combination of freshly shaved wood and tar from the corking. But Tommy saw me there and we were off again. The boys had brought some chocolate so we sat in 'our' hut eating it. We decided that we would give ourselves special names: Bertie became Ertie, Tommy became Ommy and I became Illy.

They said that I should go back to their house for tea, and I agreed although I knew my mother would be angry and wonder where I was. Their house was opposite the golf course, and was a beautiful red brick semi-detached with a garden all around and black-painted iron railings surrounding it. The large front garden had a lawn, mature trees and was full of flowers. We went straight into the kitchen where the boys' mother was cooking. It was a homely south-facing kitchen bathed in sunlight which caught the rows of copper saucepans hanging above the coal range. There was a smell of fresh yeast and baking. The kitchen seemed to be full of animals, at least two dogs and several cats all living peacefully together. The mother, Mrs Stebbings, was a striking woman and very friendly. She made us cups of tea and gave us slices of her newly baked bread. How I wished she was my mother, but I suppose all children think that, even though it made me feel very guilty in bed that night. The boys slept together in an upstairs room which overlooked the golf course and from which they could see their father's boatyard by the harbour. I didn't want to leave, and it was only when Mrs Stebbings asked if my mother wouldn't be wondering where I was, that I reluctantly set off.

We met every day after that, sometimes playing by the harbour, sometimes walking up through the woods towards Blythburgh, sometimes on the beach with the dogs, but best of all, playing soldiers in the marshy area between Walberwsick and Dunwich. Here the reeds and grasses grow tall, much taller than young boys, and this secret land is dissected by narrow paths and waterways. For hours we would plan battles and enact them in this wilderness, running for miles – unseen through the reeds to carry out an audacious ambush. Then we would collapse laughing onto the warm, sandy soil. One day, after a long and gruelling battle, as we sat by the water, Ertie said:

"My dad reckons there will be real war soon."

"So does mine," I replied remembering the talk over breakfast that morning about Spain and Hitler.

"My dad says that Kaiser Willie is a warmonger."

Well, I didn't know who this Kaiser Willie person was, but I did know what my father kept saying about Adolf Hitler, so I replied, "My dad says that Hitler is trouble and that the more we let him get away with, the worse it'll be for us in the long run."

Ommy, who hadn't really been listening, asked, "Who is this Hitler chap?"

"Everybody knows who Adolf Hitler is," I replied.

"Well I don't," Ommy said. "Come on let's carry on."

Occasionally the war games became too real and I became frightened. Ertie was brilliant at disguise and during one game I came across him lying on the bank, his head in the water. I really thought he was dead, and I dragged him out while beginning to panic. He acted quite dead and I began shouting for Ommy. Then all of a sudden he jumps up, and says, "Only acting, Illy. I knew it would frighten you."

I didn't find it at all funny and I was soon running back along the beach towards the safety of my parents' hut. I told them all about my new friends, and tried to get them to meet, but it never seemed to work out. I think that they thought I had made them up.

Looking back I remember whispered comments between them like, "It's all a game, dear. He needs some real friends." And they did try to introduce me to various children who were on holiday in Southwold, but I found them all so dull and goody-good compared to Ertie and Ommy. Occasionally, as we were sitting in the beach hut I would catch a glimpse of the boys, maybe with their mother or with the dogs, and I would call my parents to come and see them, but when we looked again they had gone, and I had to run along the beach to catch up with them. So they never did meet.

The holiday seemed to be going on forever; time was suspended and the clocks stood still. Then suddenly the spell was broken and time doubled its pace to catch up with its idle moment. It started when my mother told me not to wear a particular shirt, because she had washed and ironed it ready for London. London! The very name shook me, but I realised that I had only one day left. I ran around to the Stebbings house and caught them all at breakfast. The father, an enormous man both tall and broad, with a full beard was just leaving to cycle over to his boatyard. We decided to picnic on the sandy beach taking the dogs with us, and I ran back to tell my parents that I would not be having lunch with them that day. Then we met up beneath the lighthouse and walked along the wide expanse of sand until we all found a spot we liked. Mrs Stebbings was with us and she dozed as we made sandcastles. I clearly remember her voice, soft, melodious and suffused with a delightful Suffolk burr.

"Oh, William, if only we could look into the future. Where will we all be next year or the year after?"

I replied that my parents had booked the same house in Southwold for next summer. She laughed. "I didn't mean that,

William. I just wonder what will happen to all of us. Happiness is so fragile, and just as warm summer inevitably turns to icy winter, so …"

At that moment Ertie and Ommy came running over with the dogs telling me that they had found part of a ship's mast further along the beach, so I never discovered what Mrs Stebbings was thinking. When we came back, she had prepared lunch and we sat around eating and talking about next summer.

After lunch we swam, and it was then that I became frightened again. Mrs Stebbings had come with her swimming costume under her dress and we all started to play in the surf. Then she began to walk out into the sea, but backwards and all the time looking at me and beckoning me on. I followed until the water was up to my neck, never doubting for a moment that she would help me return, but the further I went, the further away she seemed. Then a wave knocked me over and, although I could swim, I became quite alarmed and struggled to get back towards the beach. Several times I was knocked down, and my eyes were smarting with sand and salt, and each time I fell, I found myself being pulled further out to sea.

I began to scream for help, and luckily Ertie who was swimming nearby came to my rescue. I probably was not in real danger, but I was very frightened. What was really strange was that I went I got back to our place on the beach, Mrs Stebbings was sitting there.

"I thought you were way out there in the waves," I said to her once I had stopped coughing. She just smiled. I don't have to tell you that I never mentioned a word about this to my parents.

That was the last day. Never have I wanted a day to last so long, but inevitably we had to say goodbye. I desperately wanted my parents to meet the boys and Mrs Stebbings, but as we walked past the beach hut, it was shut. My parents had gone to pack, so I asked the boys and their mother to come to the house, but they refused. So we said goodbye, there, by the hut. We hugged and promised to write and see each other the following summer. Then, early the next morning, we left that lovely place.

I wrote a Christmas card addressed to: 'The Stebbings Family, near the golf course, Southwold, Suffolk' as I didn't have their real address. But I never got a reply. Then in July we went back to Southwold, but everything had changed. The weather was bad and the waves too big for swimming; even the beach hut seemed cold and dirty while by the lighthouse, the wind howled against the windows of our little house.

As soon as I could, I went around to the Stebbings house, but to my horror it was all closed up and deserted. The beautifully kept gardens were full of weeds and long grass, the shining black railings were rusted and broken, the door to the kitchen stood open and inside all was dereliction. Tears welled in my eyes as I went around the house calling for Ertie and Ommy, but there was no reply. The house looked as if nobody had lived there for years and every piece of furniture, all the copper pans, everything had gone. With tears streaming down my face, I ran back to my parents and told them about my tragedy.

"Come on, darling," my mother said taking me in her arms. "This summer you need some real friends. You were so lonely last summer."

"Real friends," I howled. "Ertie and Ommy were real friends, my only friends."

"They weren't really real, darling."

"What do you mean?"

"Well, you know you made them up. We never saw them."

"Made them up," I sobbed quite uncontrollably. "No! No! That's not true."

After some persuasion, my parents agreed to walk over to the house and see where the Stebbings actually lived. We walked along the front, past the Seamen's Mission, the waves sending up cascades of fine spray across our path and came to the deserted house. The metal front gate was creaking as it swung in the wind, and my parents were very reluctant to go on. At that point a neighbour came across the road and my father asked about the Stebbings family.

"It's many years since they lived here, and the house belongs to some relative in Australia. Friendly with my parents, they were, a nice family mark you. It was a real tragedy though what happened to them."

I found it difficult to understand what she was saying. "What tragedy?" I asked.

"Well, first the father having that heart attack …"

"What heart attack?" I shouted.

"Dropped dead in his own boatyard, he did, and not a day over 45. That was in, let's see, about 1912. Then the tragedy of the boys, both of them mark you, was all too much for the mother."

"What happened to them?" I asked fighting back my tears.

"Albert, he was the oldest, killed on the Somme in the summer of 1916. Terrible period that, all our families suffered that summer. Then a year later, Thomas fell at Arras. Terrible it was. We could hear Mrs Stebbings wailing at night like a wounded animal."

"What happened to her?" my mother asked.

"Walked out into the sea."

"No, no!" I sobbed.

"A cold autumn day, late at night; out she walked and straight into the sea. The tragedies were just too much for her; she had no desire to live."

For days I lay on my bed, listening to the wind howling and the rain rattling the windows, weeping and sobbing. I was not at all concerned that they had all died some 20 years earlier, I was just devastated at the loss of my only friends. It was a terrible summer. During the second week, the weather improved a little, although it was still cold, and I did meet some new friends, but I returned again and again to the places where we had played, the long reeds, the boatyards, the beach. I didn't see them although I think for just a moment I glimpsed Ertie looking at me across the water, but when I looked again it was just the wind in the bull rushes. We never returned to Southwold as a family. In 1938 we went to Scotland as my father had bought a car and he wanted to 'motor' somewhere. Then came the War.

I did see the boys again, both of them. I saw Bertie just before El Alamein. I came across him on the morning of the second day when we were advancing. He was behind a small sand dune, lying beside me, and he wished me good luck. He brought me good luck, because many of the men were killed but I was unscathed. I've seen quite a lot of Tommy recently too. He's been visiting me here. He came back yesterday in his bloody uniform and upset the whole ward. I told him to go away and not to frighten my friends, but he seemed to hang around for ages.

"It's time for your medicine now, William," the nurse said.

# In the Loggia Dei Lanzi

"Just look at the result of your great idea! It's sweltering out there; it's dusty, it's noisy, it's a filthy hotel if you can call it that. All because of some romantic idea, some feeble attempt to relive your youth!"

"Coming to see Florence is hardly a 'feeble attempt'; thousands of people come to Florence to see the art every week."

"Not with young children they don't."

"That's just an excuse. It's your total lack of interest in art, that's the reason you don't want to come to … Be quiet Daniel, and leave your brother alone!"

"They're bored and they're fed up with you and your half-baked ideas. Why couldn't we have stayed at Camaggiore for another week?"

"Camaiore. Not Camaggiore."

"Oh yes, clever aren't we? Let everyone know that we speak Italian. Well that's about all you can do, and even that isn't as good as it used to be, or so you keep on telling me."

"Can we go to the beach, Daddy?"

"There isn't a beach here. Daddy has brought us to some ghastly hot, noisy dump which he calls 'artistic'."

"You know I hate beach holidays. We agreed that we would spend a few days in Florence and you accepted … Do stop whingeing, John, we'll go out soon and …"

"And what? Look at some pictures? God, just look at you, Martin Graves, you are really one of the world's great failures."

"Not in front of the children, Sal, please."

"Go to your room, boys, we'll go out in a few moments. Yes, a real failure. You looked so awful on the beach; fat and white and bald. God alive, I've tried to keep my looks but you … No wonder the Italians felt sorry for me."

"I've been trying to diet you know that."

"A fat lot of good that does. I realised right away that the 'diet' was just a way of placating me, and as soon as you've had your 'diet' you're back to the bar drinking pints with your mates, or customers or cronies or whatever name you like to give them."

"I knew you would bring the argument around to the pub sooner or later."

"Well, it's a fiasco isn't it. Why can't you admit that everything you've ever tried to do has ended in failure."

"The family, is that failure?"

"I stay with you only because of the boys. The moment they no longer need us both, although it's difficult to see how they ever need you, I'm off. You know that."

"Things might get better."

"Pigs might fly, but I'm telling you I'm off and it's no idle threat. I reckon another seven years of hell, no that's too positive a word, let's call it purgatory where nobody knows whether they're coming or going; another seven years and I'm off and you can do all your dreaming by yourself."

Martin could feel his anger rising, his heart was beating as if to a South American rhythm and he could feel that ominous pain creeping across his chest as if someone unseen was tightening a metal belt around his torso; he was sweating profusely in the heat and patches of damp were appearing on his shirt.

"Why don't you let me go and …"

"Go where? Back to your grotty little pub that you call 'the business'? You can't even run that at a profit."

"You are a foul mouthed …" But Martin never finished his sentence and as his wife's words, "You are really one of the world's great failures," rang around his head, he unlocked the grubby cream painted door of the hotel bedroom, walked past the only toilet on the landing, down the stairs, past the owner who was pretending not to have heard anything of the row, and out onto the dirty and noisy boulevard which ran behind the railway station.

He boarded the first bus that came past; it did not matter where it was going, but he noticed that it was signed to the Piazza della Repubblica. Much of what Sal had said had been true, and the real pain in his life was coming to terms with the knowledge that he was indeed a failure. It was not so much that he was personally a failure; he still retained a sense of fun and humour and he still had many friends, but he had never really discovered in life that which he could do well.

He often thought about the distant past, because in many ways it was better than the present, although he recognised that in these times of recession and hardship many people probably felt the same. And it was this desire to relive the past which had brought him back to Florence, which he had vainly hoped he might share with his family.

"Maybe the boys were too young," he said aloud. "Maybe we should have stayed by the sea."

He noticed an attractive young girl looking at him, but with his balding head and lumbering figure he was sadly aware that it was out of curiosity not attraction. And yet he had been young and he had been young in Florence, but since then everything seemed to have gone wrong. His years at art school has not resulted in a scholarship to the Royal College of Art as he had hoped, but had led instead to three impoverished years trying to sell his paintings while doing a number of menial part-time jobs to keep alive.

It was one of these jobs, selling art materials at an art fair that had led to a full-time post with a company distributing artists' colours and brushes, and for a while, with some money in his pocket and a new wife, life seemed sweet. Eventually even that had gone wrong. The company was taken over; younger, more dynamic men were promoted and Martin was left as a travelling salesman. He did not even have time to paint, nor any inclination. The crunch had come five years ago when he had been called into the managing director's office and sacked with little ceremony and few regrets on either side. He had known for some time that this was coming; the art materials business was changing dramatically with new promotional schemes and modern advertising methods. Famous artists were being invited to give demonstrations before hundreds of eager amateurs and the role of the ex-art college student with a five-year-old Ford Fiesta and a suitcase full of brushes, oil paints, boxes of watercolours and sketchbooks no longer existed. Nevertheless, it was a blow, especially with two very young sons, but the dream of running a country pub had long beckoned and now, armed with a fair redundancy payment, was the ideal opportunity.

Needless to say, the pub had also gone wrong. Martin laughed out aloud in the bus, causing a number of people to turn around and mutter, "E pazzo, questo," but he had to laugh.

Why had he said, "Needless to say?"

It was as if he had accepted that everything he did went wrong. In fact, it was not entirely his fault that it had gone wrong. Sal hated serving behind the bar and refused to do so, forcing Martin to employ staff, one of whom had stolen most of the profits for their first year. The children also hated the pub; on the one hand the 'gentry' of the village refused to accept the publican and his family socially, while the village children considered them to be 'Londoners'. The pub was actually beginning to make some small profits, and at least it was a roof over their heads, but Martin was left alone to run it. The so-called 'partnership' in marriage had long since been dissolved. He thought of selling up, but prices of public houses had collapsed and selling up would have wiped out their capital.

As the bus turned, Martin saw himself reflected in the round mirror by the driver's seat. It was not, he had to admit, a pretty sight, made worse by the distortion of the concave glass. Sal was perfectly right, he was, at 18 stone, grossly overweight, but he had tried to diet and it was some comfort that he had lost nearly a stone since the autumn. *But,* he reflected, *what was the purpose of dieting?* It meant more than just eating less; it entailed eating with the family rather than at the bar, confining himself to one pint spread over the whole evening rather than the usual eight or so, of which many were bought by his customers. And, worst of all, it meant going up to the family rooms late at night sober and unready to face the hostility and criticism at which Sal was so expert. It was not that he came upstairs drunk, but he had drunk and that provided a comforting barrier against the realities of life. He had also bought a cycling machine, but the effort in the morning, especially when there was just the slightest touch of a headache, was enough to make him feel quite sick. The experiment had not lasted long; the machine being sold through the local newspaper. Being overweight was not pleasant; he hated the image and the constant effort it required to do even the simplest of tasks; but being sober at night was worse.

Then he caught sight of the railway station, a masterpiece of the 1930s design and remembered the thrill of arriving in a new country. For a young man who had just left school and whose family background in small terraced house in Enfield had not prepared him for living anywhere other than in the London suburbs, the excitement of Italy was overwhelming. This was 1997, a year he would never forget. He had seen a job advertising teaching English to Italian students at the British Institute of Florence and to his great surprise his application had been successful. Now here he was, taking a taxi to an unknown family where he was to live for the next year. Fear and pleasurable anticipation vied for control of his emotions. He remembered so clearly his first days with the family speaking no Italian, but quickly learning with the help of the young children. For a moment he imagined that the girl who was looking at him could even be Laura, the eight-year-old who had laughed at his bad pronunciation and had unwittingly taught him so much Italian, but then he realised that by now she would be married and with her own eight-year-old. He wondered whether the family still lived in Florence; maybe if he had a moment he would look them up in the telephone book.

The bus passed the station and for a fleeting moment Martin caught sight of the school where he had taught English, as a complete novice, to a trusting and respectful group of young Italians. He smiled when he looked back at his amateurism; today EFL teaching is so regimented that unless you have a qualification you cannot teach. Martin knew this first hand as he had thought of returning to English teaching before the disastrous move to the pub, but a few preliminary investigations proved that he had no chance of getting a job. And yet it had all worked out; his pupils had come to like and trust him, and he had come to enjoy their company.

The bus drew into the Piazza della Repubblica and all the passengers got off. As Martin descended he felt the warm sunshine on his back. The bank where he had held his account was still there and he felt for a moment that he was going there, the cheque from the school in his hand. Instead he headed towards the Piazza della Signoria. Memories flooded back: the grim facade of the Palazzo Vecchio which had so impressed him the first time he had seen it, the shop which sold postcards, old photographs and artists' materials still standing on the opposite side of the square, unchanged in any respect: And to the south, the Loggia dei Lanzi.

Martin was reluctant to go into the Loggia, sitting instead by the Neptune Fountain. It was here that he used to meet Francesca Castagnoli, the love of his youth, indeed of his life. One autumn morning he had walked into his early evening class and there she was, seated in the front, a dark haired girl aged 18 with classic Italian looks. She was maybe not beautiful in the traditional sense of the word, but certainly striking. Her almost black hair fell richly over her shoulders emphasising her high cheekbones and sculpted face; her eyes were dark, outlined by long eyelashes and heavy eyebrows which rose elegantly in a curving arch. Her mouth was full, sensual and extremely expressive, reflecting her every mood, which was most of the time radiantly happy. Martin remembered how, on that first day, he had found it difficult to talk to the whole class, his attention constantly returning to the newcomer in the front. For the whole of the following week he had thought about her, and everywhere he went he thought he could see her. And at the next class, she had noticed him, greeting him with an exquisite, "Ciao, come stai", before the lesson began.

They began to meet on Saturdays and Sunday afternoons, arranging a rendezvous in the Loggia dei Lanzi. Then they would visit an art gallery followed by a dance on a Sunday afternoon in one of the many dancing clubs, or even take a bus into one of the hill villages that surround Florence. As a relationship it had been bliss, even though it had developed slowly against the background of Francesca's strict Catholic upbringing. Her parents were pharmacists and owned as successful business where Francesca worked some Saturdays. They had at first been wary of him, but had come to like him and invited him to spend weekends on their farm in the Tuscan countryside. These indeed had been weekends in Paradise. "Paradise is not a place," Martin said out loud, "it's a state of mind. I found Paradise and I lost it forever. I threw it away."

The young lovers seated around the fountain took no notice of his monologue.

"No responsibilities to anyone, no financial worries, no dependents, no wife to destroy romance, no worries about growing old or fat or ugly or bald or repulsive to the young."

He remembered the period of torment when, in the summer of 1998, he had had to decide whether to go back to his art school place in England or stay in Italy, possibly even marrying Francesca. He had taken what seemed at the time the right, the sensible decision, but in retrospect he had often wondered what would have happened if he had stayed in Florence. He would have continued teaching English, maybe he would have been successful as a painter; Francesca, unlike Sal, always encouraged his art. But then again, maybe that marriage would also have gone wrong; she was very young and had not even started her university course in pharmacy. However, Martin liked to think that somehow it might have worked, and he often day dreamed about the Italian family man that he might have become. It was as if he needed a little ray of hope, albeit impossible hope, to make the present more tolerable.

As the water played in the fountain, Martin became aware that he could smell that unique scent of water tumbling in sunlight, and he could feel a fine wet mist on his face. Other smells became evident; cooking from a little trattoria nearby, the perfume of the girl embracing her boyfriend by the fountain. Martin realised that for many years he had completely lost his sense of smell, apart from the most obvious and pungent smell of stale beer and tobacco in the bar each morning. He left the fountain and somewhat reluctantly made his way towards the Loggia. The memories of their meetings came flooding back; they always arranged to meet 'in the Loggia dei Lanzi' usually by Cellini's statue of Perseus. He walked slowly across the Piazza and into the deep shade of the Loggia. A group of tourists were being told about the statue.

"Perseus is holding up the head of Medusa so that everyone in the Piazza can see it. Perseus slew his enemies by turning them to stone. Now follow me to the next statue which is by Donatello ..."

The group dissolved away leaving one girl standing looking up at Cellini's masterpiece. As Martin approached the base of the statute, the girl, still with her back to him, said quietly, "Ciao, Prof. Molto Grave."

Francesca had always made a play on his surname, which in Italian, spelt without the final 's' meant serious or solemn. She had often referred to him in class as 'il Professore Grave' sometimes adding 'molto', which meant 'very', as a corruption of Martin. Then she slowly turned around, smiling broadly and extending her arms to embrace him. Francesca had not changed at all; her hair was as dark and lustrous as ever, hanging in heavy waves to her shoulders; her intense dark eyes were still as deep as shaded pools set off by her light olive coloured complexion; her mouth, extended in a sensual smile, was as beautiful and expressive as it had been thirty years ago.

Martin could say nothing. He fell into her arms as if drawn towards her by a magnetic force and for what seemed an eternity they embraced without saying a word. Martin had often noted how, as middle age crept up, couples rarely physically expressed emotion in public, as if embarrassed by their image, fearing to look silly in front of the young. Now, in this moment of extraordinary and confusing emotion, he felt no such constraints. Their kiss was long and passionate. Finally, holding her at arm's length and looking into her eyes, he said, in perfect Italian, "It's quite unbelievable. You haven't changed since the last embrace at the railway station in July 1998."

"Thursday, July 21," she added. "The day you left me; for better or for worse."

"For worse, for worse."

"The worst was that you never came back."

"I tried, but I was a poor art student and holidays were spent working to pay my way. I planned to return, but … well, life went in another direction. You must have hated me for that."

"No, I understood."

"But why did you stop writing to me? Suddenly your letters stopped and my umbilical cord with Italy was severed."

"My own life changed and …"

"Are you happy? That's what matters."

"I've found peace," Francesca replied enigmatically. "And you?"

"No, I cannot say that I'm happy, nor that I've found peace."

"A difficult wife, two children, financial problems …"

"How did you know that?"

Francesca smiled sweetly. "Maybe I just guessed. Anyway let's talk about the past; that's when we both found real happiness."

They strolled hand in hand amongst the tourists in the Piazza before Martin suggested eating together in a trattoria which they had enjoyed so many years ago. To Martin's surprise it was still there, although now called ‘Da Romano’ rather than ‘Da Beppo’.

“Things change more slowly in Italy,” Francesca remarked. “It’s probably owned by Beppo’s son.”

The menu had changed little and Martin remembered Francesca’s favourite dishes. Over veal escallops and a bottle of Frascati, they talked about the past, about friends they had known together, about the weekends they had passed together in the country. They rarely mentioned the present, except to say how much better the past had been.

“You haven’t changed at all, Francesca,” Martin repeated.

“You’re not so bad yourself,” Francesca replied.

“That’s a joke. I’m old, balding, too fat.”

“But that’s not true.” She protested which made Martin feel better than he had for years. Somehow he felt the sensations of youth returning; the veal tasted like nothing he had eaten recently, the wine had a delectable sparkle and hint of fruit, quite unlike the tasteless wine he served in the pub. The whole restaurant had an exquisite combination of subtle smells, of expresso coffee, of cigars, of the rosemary in which some lamb was being roasted, of the basil in the tomato salad.

“Even being with you makes me feel younger,” Martin said removing his glasses and finding, much to his surprise, that he did not really need them. “Recently I have been feeling so very old, washed up and totally useless.”

Finally, Romano politely hinted that the restaurant was closing for the afternoon break; Martin paid the bill and went to the cloakroom. He washed his hands and face in a basin of cold water, and as he dried his face he noticed that, as well as feeling younger, he looked younger. His eyes had regained some of their old twinkle, his hair seemed a little darker, even thicker and, was it just his imagination, or did he really feel lighter, thinner, more athletic?

"It's in the mind," he said to himself. "If you feel young, you are young."

They walked arm in arm across the Ponte Vecchio and embraced in the little loggia which overlooks the river. There they stood for some time, each silently recalling the past, oblivious to the noise and bustle of the present. Then they walked to the Boboli Gardens, and sat around the fountains and strolled amongst the formal flower gardens. Once again Martin was aware of a sense of smell that for many years had deserted him; the richly scented flowers, the fresh breeze which blew off the fountains, Francesca's heady perfume. Then they took a taxi up to Piazzale Michelangelo from where the visitor has a magnificent view over the whole of Florence.

"The cathedral looks more impressive than I remember it." Martin reflected. "What's the tower in front?"

"That's the Palazzo Vecchio."

"Of course. How lovely the hills around Fiesole look in the afternoon sunlight. Do you remember our Sunday evening walks there?"

"So well. And the dancing afterwards."

"Whereabouts in Florence do you live now?"

"In a very quiet and beautiful place."

"Well," Martin insisted. "Tell me more about your home and family. Are you married?"

"Stai zitto, caro! Keep quiet and enjoy the moment," Francesca said with a radiant smile. "Don't ask so many questions." They embraced again with a long lingering kiss, both quite oblivious to the tourist coaches which come in an endless stream to view Florence from the Piazzale.

They walked down the hill towards the town centre as the sun was beginning to turn a golden ochre. Then Francesca suggested that they take a bus to San Casciano, a village outside Florence where they had often walked together in the late afternoon.

"It's beginning to get late," Martin said looking at his watch. "Maybe I ought to be thinking about getting back."

"Back to what? Your old life? No come with me; we'll walk from San Casciano and see the sunset as we used to do. It's too perfect a day to let it go; you'll never have another day like this."

The bus took them up into the hills south of Florence and left them in the small village of San Casciano outside the little Renaissance church of the Misericordia. They walked to the terrace overlooking the valley which was bathed in the golden light of a Tuscan evening, and could make out the tiny village of Sant' Andrea about two miles away.

"Maybe we should find out when the last bus returns to Florence," Martin suggested.

Francesca laughed. "You're still wedded to your old life. Let's start again and cast off everything that has happened since we last met."

"You're suggesting that we stay together forever? That I should just disappear and never see my family again?" Martin said thoughtfully. "Maybe I should; I can hardly say that I'd miss them."

"Come, let's walk across the valley and try to relive the past, even if it's just an illusion."

The path to Sant'Andrea was a well-used public footpath, popular with weekend hikers. On this mid-week summer's evening however it was deserted and all was silent except for the sound of the birds in the trees. They walked slowly and every now and then indulged themselves in a long and passionate embrace. Martin's physical passions were returning after a long winter's sleep: he had attempted intercourse with Sal while in Camaiore, but the result had been the usual disaster, with bitter recriminations on both sides. Now the beautiful presence of Francesca was arousing a passion that he had thought long-lost.

"Do you remember this path?" she asked him during one of their embraces.

"I certainly remember walking here with you after work on summer evenings just like this."

"But something special happened near here."

"Was it really here that we first made love?"

"Of course, it was over there in that little wood. Let's go down this path; I want to share with you my deepest secret."

The thought of being unfaithful to Sal had not crossed Martin's mind for many years, as the opportunity had never arisen. He had sometimes wondered whether taking a lover might solve the problems of his marriage, but his commitments to the family and the pub had made even such a thought an impracticality. Now, presented with the opportunity all doubts evaporated in the heat of his desire. Francesca led him down a path which led into a small wood of pine trees. The ground beneath his feet was soft and springy and the air was full of the rich resinous perfume of the pines.

Against all expectations, Sal and the children had a lovely day. The owner of the hotel directed them to the public swimming pool where they spent the morning before taking a bus to the Piazza della Signoria where the boys ate two pizzas each in a busy pizzeria very close to the restaurant where

Martin and Francesca were eating lunch. Then they walked over the Ponte Vecchio, passing within a few feet of the couple embracing passionately in the little loggia overlooking the river. On returning late to their hotel, Sal did not really expect to find that Martin had returned. She felt that she had been too hard on him, and had been for several years, and that he needed a day by himself to think and reconsider his life. Having put the boys to bed, she told the concierge that her husband would likely return late, and then gave herself the luxury of an early night. The next morning brought no news of Martin, and later in the day she telephoned the British Consulate explaining her problem. The Consulate's advice was for her to wait another night, but if he had not returned by the morning she would be accompanied to the police by an interpreter. In the meantime, they took Martin's full details and description to circulate to the police.

"There have been no fatalities in road accidents over the last 48 hours," the Police Inspector said leafing through some papers. "Most Florentines are either by the sea or in the mountains, and the traffic is very light. A couple of tourists taken to hospital and, oh yes, one heart attack victim." Sal looked tense for a moment. "But he was an American and we have his details."

"Have you circulated Mr Graves' description to all police stations?" the Consul asked.

"Yes, as a matter of course, the details of missing persons go to all police stations throughout Italy. But you said, Signora, that your husband had contacts in Florence."

"Many years ago he taught here at the British Institute and he certainly had friends then, but I don't think he has kept in touch."

"But he could have found them again."

"It is possible."

"What were their names?"

"I really don't know. He talked of a girl called Francesca …"

"There must be thousands of Francesca's in Florence."

"I could probably find her name and address amongst his papers back in England."

Much to Sal's distress, she was advised by the Consulate to take her family back to England on their booked flight and, after some delay in retrieving the car at the airport caused by the fact that Martin had disappeared with the parking lot ticket, they reached home. Finding Francesca's surname proved easy and Sal was soon passing the information on to the British Consulate in Florence.

It was about midday the following day before the Consul phoned to inform her that they had contacted the Castagnoli family.

"I'm afraid this lead has proved unfruitful," the Consul said. "We spoke to Francesca Castagnoli's brother, who appeared reluctant to talk either about his sister or your husband. This is slightly embarrassing and probably has no relevance to your husband's disappearance, but after some persuasion Dr Castagnoli told us that his sister had committed suicide in the autumn of 1998. Apparently she was five months pregnant and … I don't know quite how to put this, Mrs Graves but it would appear that your husband was her only boyfriend and was certainly, well would certainly have been, the father."

"My God, Martin never mentioned that." Sal gasped.

"It appears that he never knew."

"Even worse. But is there any connection between this and his disappearance?"

"The police think not. Dr Castagnoli is a distinguished surgeon who wouldn't have dreamt of exacting a revenge. Moreover, he didn't even know that your husband was in Florence. In the meantime, the police are continuing their search and if there is any news we will let you know."

Pietro Ruggieri disliked the police. Many years ago, in fact he could be precise about the date, it was in the autumn of 1998, he had found a young girl in his woods while cutting fuel for his fire. She appeared to be sleeping peacefully, and he carried her back to the farmhouse and called the police. That was a big mistake. When they arrived they pronounced the girl dead and began to act in such a way as to make Pietro think they suspected him of foul play. They ransacked the house and the barn taking away all his insecticides for examination, and it was only after the girl's parents found her note and came to identify the body that the police, almost reluctantly, took the pressure off him. She had taken poison from her parents' pharmacy and not from Pietro's barn as the police suspected. But some of his neighbours, especially that old witch Signora Rapacelli, still whisper that he was somehow involved.

Poor girl! So beautiful and so peaceful in death. How could her lover have deserted her like that? Well, this body wasn't beautiful nor peaceful. It must have been there for months, and was half eaten by the foxes and dogs of the area. Probably a man, but Pietro did not care about its sex nor how it died, and he certainly had no intention of calling the police. He dug a deep grave in the soft earth beneath the trees, pushed the mortal remains of Martin Graves in and covered them thoroughly with earth and leaves.

Martin Graves became yet another name on the list of missing persons, suspended forever in a bureaucratic Purgatory neither alive nor dead.

# Lieutenant Leaman

It is strange how a single purchase, often made on the spur of the moment, or at least without too much consideration, can transform one's life, often for the better, but sometimes for the worse. There are cases of investors putting small sums of money into new companies being set up by friends or neighbours, and ending up with a stake in the company worth millions of pounds. Sometimes, however, such a decision can be made without realising the implications at the time; for example, the cases of people buying priceless paintings or important pieces of Chinese porcelain in local junk shops, and only years later appreciating their value. The case of Michael Prescott is less fortunate, although it also started with a single, and on the surface at least, an uncomplicated purchase in a local antique shop.

Michael Prescott could be described as a successful, self-made man; he was brought up in very modest circumstances in London, went to local school becoming the only pupil in his year to get to university, which he achieved by dint of hard work and determination. He studied Economics at Manchester before joining a life assurance company as a salesman. His progress was swift, becoming senior salesman and eventually regional manager. By the time he was 45, he held an important supervisory role which took him to the main London office situated near Baker Street, to the administrative centre at Swindon and to a number of regional offices in the South West.

He was known to be calm, rational and 'a safe pair of hands' during a crisis. Married, with three children, he had recently moved from Fulham to Newbury where he believed the standard of living and education were both better. His wife, Jane, was a keen horseman and had welcomed the move to one of the centres of the equestrian business in England and had quickly found a fulfilling part-time job as a riding instructor some 15 minutes by car from the house.

Built around 1885, the large double fronted Victorian villa had all the space and elegance that they both wanted, and in London would have been outside their financial reach. There was much renovation work still to be done, but they were tackling it room by room, and had plans to open up the large roof space into a playroom and study for the children. In all, despite some extra time spent on the train, Michael was extremely pleased that they had made the bold decision to leave London.

The town of Newbury appealed to both Michael and Jane and they enjoyed walking by the river and the 'village' feeling which the centre had retained, despite development all around. Behind the church situated by the River Kennett, they found a fascinating junk shop full of pottery, brass, pictures, frames and old household equipment. Jane was particularly interested in old kitchen appliances and had designed their new kitchen in a Victorian country style; Michael's interest lay in First World War memorabilia. This interest had been stimulated by his grandfather who had fought on the Somme and who had regaled the young Michael with stories of heroism and death.

On his grandfather's death, Michael was delighted to discover that he had been left all his War mementos including pay books, photographs, a fascinating diary and jagged fragments of shells. This had formed the basis of a collection which had grown steadily over the years, and it was often in junk shops such as the one by the River Kennett that the best things could be discovered: This late Saturday afternoon on a dank, rainy November day was no exception. Michael was interested to discover a medallion, about four and a half inches in diameter, bearing the inscription: 'He Died For Freedom and Honour' and the representation of Britannia and the Lion. In a box on the right was inscribed the name Arthur Edward Leaman. Michael knew that these medallions had been coined during the First World War to commemorate the fallen. Having bought it for very little he decided that it might be interesting to discover the circumstances of Leaman's death, but how many times over the next two years was he to wish that he had never discovered the medallion, leaving it buried as it was under a pile of 'Illustrated London News' from the 1930s.

The next six months were hectic both for Michael and his wife; the life assurance company was the process of retraining its salesman creating a huge amount of work for Michael and the managerial staff, while at home Michael and Jane were themselves working on two of the upstairs bedrooms. There was no time to think about researching the medallion and it lay, almost forgotten, in a glass cabinet. One Friday evening Michael returned from work to find his wife at the kitchen table polishing a small silver photograph frame which she had bought in a silver shop in Hungerford that afternoon. It was very tarnished as the shop owner had not had time to clean it but Jane felt that, as a result of its poor condition, she had got it for a very keen price. The silver marks bore the code for 1912 and in it was a faded colour photograph of a girl on a horse. As Jane removed the photograph, another much older photograph fell out of the frame. It was of a young British officer in First World War uniform.

Handing the photograph to her husband, Jane said with a laugh, "I seem to have bought something for your collection as well as for myself."

The photograph was in good condition having been protected from the light for many years, and it revealed a young man with a strong, aquiline face but sensitive dark eyes. As with most men of that period, he sported a moustache which was neatly trimmed.

"Looks as if he was in the Royal Wiltshire Fusiliers," Michael commented before turning it over. "My God! What a coincidence! You'll never believe this, Jane, but the photograph is inscribed 'Arthur Edward Leaman 1895–1915. Lieutenant, Royal Wiltshire Fusiliers'."

"Who was Leaman?"

"Don't you remember, the medallion we bought in the autumn was to Arthur Edward Leaman. It just seems such a strange coincidence that this frame should have contained his photograph. It's almost unbelievable."

Prompted by the strange coincidence, Michael set about to find out more about the dead soldier but the lead appeared to peter out at this point; Michael could find no Leamans in the local telephone directory, and the junk shop where he had found the medallion were unable to tell him about its provenance. However, he made time to go to the library to search out some further information. In the 'Roll of Honour' of the officers of Royal Wiltshire Fusiliers he found a photograph of Leaman, in fact the same photograph as the one in the frame, and a very brief entry listing his education, the names of his parents and the fact that he had died near Bethune on 29 March 1915. Interestingly enough, his father had been a regular soldier, a retired Major of the Royal Wiltshire Fusiliers and the family had lived in Newbury. Michael found the book intensely depressing; out of its musty pages the photographs of the bold young men of 1914 stared resolutely at the reader, as if defying death. All had been well educated and had mostly died shortly after joining up, their long and arduous preparation for life wasted in a matter of weeks.

Leaman had been destined to follow his father's career in the Army; he had gone to Sandhurst, been commissioned in May 1914 just before the War started and had been promoted to First Lieutenant the following February. Unlike most of the other entries, there were no details about his actual death nor was there the normal commendation by his senior officer. Otherwise the entry on Lt Leaman was depressingly like the many others in the vellum-bound book. Later that day Michael wrote to the Commonwealth War Graves Commission in Maidenhead requesting information as to where Leaman was buried and, with the Commission's usual efficiency, he received a swift response. Leaman lay in Plot 5, Row L, Grave 7 in Petit Beaucourt British Cemetery near Bethune.

Michael put Leaman out of his mind during the family's summer holiday which was spent camping, swimming and canoeing in the Ardeche region of France, but on the way back to England, a sudden compulsion took hold of him, and taking a turning off the Autoroute des Anglais which runs up to Calais, he made a brief detour towards the cemetery of Petit Beaucourt. The cemetery, surrounded by a stone wall, was set on a slight hill; behind it a small wood had grown densely shielding it from the noise and anachronistic intrusion of the motorway. The road up to the cemetery was sunk between steep banks, making it appear larger than it actually was and fortress-like in its austerity.

As they approached, the summer storm which had been threatening all the way since Arras, broke behind them. To the west, the sky remained clear but to the east deeply purple rain clouds were building up, higher and higher into the sky and vertical streaks of dark ultramarine told of heavy rain to come. A great rainbow soared above the cemetery as Michael entered it alone, his family preferring to remain in the shelter of the car. The First World War cemeteries present a strange combination of tranquillity and infinite sadness, and this was no exception, but the sound of approaching thunder coupled with the shrill shrieks of alarmed birds in the woods behind added a sinister element. Michael quickly located the grave which was identical to the others, but somehow he had a feeling, possibly quite irrational, that Leaman's death had been unusual. He was keen to leave the cemetery, and as they drove back towards Calais he wondered what it was that had drawn him towards that place. Whatever it had been, it caused them to miss their ferry, and because it was a busy evening they had to wait several hours before they could cross.

Some months later, nearly a year since he first bought the medallion, Michael was decorating one of the front rooms of the house. It was an overcast Saturday and he was alone in the house. As he undercoated the woodwork around the window he was aware that a young man was looking up intently at the window. He was wearing a greatcoat and khaki cap, a fashion currently in vogue with young people. At first Michael took little notice, but when he put his paintbrush down to have a sip of tea, he noticed that the figure had disappeared. Yet when he resumed work he was once again aware that he was being observed. He went downstairs to the front door and looked out, but the street was deserted.

About an hour later, when the daylight had almost gone, he heard the unusual sound of the old doorbell ringing in the hall. This was a small bell on a spring which originally had been connected to a door-pull, but now could only be rung from the inside by climbing a ladder and pulling it. Michael assumed that the children, who enjoyed doing this, had returned from the sports hall and went downstairs to greet them. As he came down the stairs to the hall, he saw the bell moving apparently by itself, and also noticed the silhouette of a figure against the stained glass panel of the door. He knew that the person outside could not be making the bell ring, as they had disconnected the bell-pull, replacing it with a more audible electric bell. Then he noticed that the figure looked similar to the young man he had seen earlier, wearing a greatcoat and military style cap. He opened the door, keen to confront the young man, but no one was there. He looked up and down the road, but again it was deserted.

By now he was trembling with illogical fear, and his hands had become cold and stiff. Going into the kitchen, he turned on the television, that ever-present link with the rational twentieth century, and made himself a cup of tea. Just a few moments later the children arrived back with Jane who was alarmed at his appearance.

"You look terribly ill, darling. Are the paint fumes upsetting you? Why don't you go and lie down?"

When the children had gone to their rooms, he told his wife about the strange experience of the doorbell and figure, but he felt that Jane, who was keen to get the children's supper ready, was not entirely sympathetic.

For several weeks after this episode Michael brooded upon it as he drove to work. Eventually the rational side of his character triumphed and he convinced himself that it had been a strange series of coincidences which had produced such an unexpected result. Jane was convinced that the silhouette had been that of a burglar who had disappeared quickly once he realised that someone was in the house. This explanation was further reinforced in Jane's mind by an event which took place in the early hours of a stormy November morning. Both Michael and Jane liked to sleep with the bedroom windows wide open, and occasionally the draft would cause the bedroom door to spring open, as the catch needed attention. On this particular morning the wind was near gale force and the rain lashed against the window. Michael woke up just before three o'clock convinced that he had heard the front door slam shut. Then he heard footsteps up the stairs; they were the footsteps of a young person taking two steps at a time. At that moment the door blew open and for a couple of seconds Michael could make out the figure of a young man bathed in the unreal yellow light of the street lamps standing by the door and looking towards the bed. His face was somehow familiar with sharp features, a well-trimmed moustache and piercing eyes. Then he was gone, leaving

Michael unsure of whether he had really seen anything other than the dressing gown on the back of the door. Jane awoke with a start, sat up and commented yet again on the need to get the door catch fixed.

"Didn't you hear the footsteps?" Michael asked as he got up and put on his dressing gown.

"What footsteps?"

"I could swear that I heard someone coming up the stairs."

"Oh don't start that again. It makes me feel quite creepy," Jane replied as she lay down, turned over and covered herself with the duvet.

Michael went to see if either of the children had got up, then went downstairs. A section of the glass in the front door had been broken and the shattered fragments lay on the hall floor. He called Jane down and together they went around the house to see if anything had been stolen; Jane insisted on calling the police. As far as they could see, nothing had been taken and the only thing that appeared to have been touched was the cabinet in the sitting room: Its glass door stood open and the First World War medallion lay on the floor next to the photograph of Lt Leaman.

Looking at the photograph, Michael realised why the young man's face, glimpsed for a passing instant, had appeared familiar. His attempts to make Jane see that this was part of the strange coincidences and events that had taken place recently fell on deaf ears. Both she and the police were convinced that it had been a case of an attempted burglary, linked almost certainly to the earlier episode when Michael had seen a figure through the glass of the front door. When the bedroom door flew open with the wind, the burglar, fearing that he had been heard, had left quickly without taking anything.

For fear of appearing neurotic, Michael did not mention seeing the figure of the young man in the bedroom, and when he queried why a burglar should attempt to steal a medallion and photograph, the explanation offered by the police and supported by his wife, was that the cabinet would have been the first item of furniture the burglar would have noticed on opening the sitting room door. Once again over the next weeks, he was able to rationalise the events of the night, and half convinced himself that it had been attempted burglary in both cases.

The next development in a series of coincidences came, quite by chance, through one of Jane's riding pupils. Sarah Bridgeman, an eight-year-old star of the stables, lived on the other side of Newbury, and her mother, who worked as an accountant, had difficulty collecting her from the riding school at half past five. It was agreed that Jane would bring her home and the mother could collect her as soon as she was free. The arrangement worked well, and one evening the girl's grandmother accompanied her daughter to the Prescott's house.

"You don't mind if I come in, but I know this house very well," the old lady said.

"Please do, and tell me about it. I know my husband would love to know something of its history."

"Well I remember it when I was a little girl towards the end of the war – that's the Great War, of course – my mother did a lot of voluntary work and there was a couple, quite elderly I suppose, though of course to a young girl everyone over thirty looks old! Well, they had lost their only son during the War, and my mother used to come and visit. The father had been a soldier himself, though too old to fight in the War, and their world just fell apart when the news of their son's death came through. We, that's my mother and I, used to visit, bringing cakes and spending some time talking with them, just to cheer them up a bit. The father died soon afterwards; they did say he died of a broken heart, and certainly he had nothing to live for. The mother must have died a few years later because I remember she was still alive in 1920 because she gave me a little gold charm for my bracelet for my tenth birthday, which was in 1920, but we stopped coming to the house about a year later."

The old lady could not remember the name of the family, although she said it was on the tip of her tongue. She promised to let them know if she could remember it, and later that evening, when the children had gone to bed and Michael had not yet returned from work, the telephone rang. It was Mrs Bridgeman.

"I'm sorry about my mother. She does go on a bit."

"No, don't apologise. I was fascinated by what she had to say."

"She has remembered the name of the family. It was a Major and Mrs Leaman."

Jane felt the hair on the back of her neck tingling, and as she put the phone down she thought she heard the front door open and shut and Michael going straight upstairs, two at a time. Strangely, rather than going into the children's room, he appeared to enter one of the back bedrooms which they had not yet renovated. Putting the dinner into the microwave, she started to lay a tray to take into the sitting room so they could eat their dinner in front of the fire. At that moment the doorbell rang; Michael was standing in the porch.

"I'm sorry about that, but I left my keys in my other jacket."

"But I've just heard you come in. Didn't you go up to the back room?"

It was Jane's turn to feel alarmed at the evening's events which she described in detail to Michael.

"We are going to have to stop this whole business. It's upsetting both of us and I don't believe in delving into …"

"Into what?" Michael queried.

"Well, into the unknown. I think what we're doing is quite dangerous. We seem to be stirring up all sorts of events, or coincidences we can't control."

"I agree, but there must be some reason why this figure, this apparition or whatever it is, keeps returning here to this house."

"The best thing to do would be to take the photograph and the medallion back to the junk shop. Don't try to sell them, just give them back, and if they don't want them drop them into the Kennett."

Jane was quite insistent that her husband should return the medallion to the shop by the river, and the following Saturday, almost a year since he had first bought it, Michael reluctantly entered the shop with the medallion and in his pocket. Selling life assurance appeared easy compared to reselling antiques, and the shop owner expressed almost no interest in the item, even denying that he had ever sold it in the first place. Finally, after a quite heated discussion, he offered Michael a derisory amount. Angered by his failure to negotiate effectively,

Michael replied that he would rather throw the medallion into the river and invited the shop owner to watch him.

An autumn mist had descended with the late October nightfall and it was difficult to see clearly even as far as the other side of the Kennett. Michael walked to the riverbank and hurled the medallion and the photograph of Leaman which had also brought with him into the murky water, much to the amazement of the dealer who really believed that his customer had been staging an elaborate bluff. He was even more surprised by the words that this extraordinary collector uttered as he threw away part of his collection.

"Take these and leave us all in peace!"

"Quite mad," the dealer muttered to himself as he began putting up his metal shutters.

The renovation of the house was progressing quite well, and they decided that it was time to tackle one of the bedrooms at the back of the house which would originally have been a maid's room. As he was stripping the old wallpaper, Michael noticed that, while the plaster over the fireplace was solid, as he tapped the wall either side of the mantelpiece, it sounded hollow, as if he was tapping wood rather than brick and plaster. He went downstairs to his tool box, and returned with a hammer, a cold chisel and crowbar, and began stripping the old wallpaper. Soon he discovered that under the wallpaper there was some cheap wooden boarding which easily came away from the wall. He smelt a dank, musty odour as he discovered some traditional Victorian built-in shelving, which had been deliberately boarded up and wallpapered many years ago. On one of the shelves was a bundle of papers, and Michael knew before opening them that somehow they related to Leaman.

Together they looked through the papers, which at first looked rather ordinary. There was Lt Leaman's Pay Book, a copy of his commission into the Royal Wiltshire Fusiliers dated May 1914, a telegram notifying the parents of his death in March 1915 and some of his personal possessions which had been returned by his Captain. Then, in a separate bundle, were some letters addressed to Major and Mrs Leaman and written, not from France but from addresses in Southern England.

It was here that Michael and Jane Prescott began to discover the cause of the mystery surrounding Leaman's death. The most revealing came from a Capt. Jackman, was dated October 1917 and written from Bristol.

'Dear Major and Mrs Leaman,

Thank you for your letter and your concern about my health. I am pleased to say that I am making a good recovery, and although I am told I will never be able to walk without a stick, I feel that I have suffered less than many.

This is a difficult letter for me to write, and although I have been discharged from the Army, I still would ask you to keep any information it contains entirely confidential. Your suspicions are correct and it would be dishonest for me to deny the truth as I know it. Arthur, who was a dear and loyal friend, died in unusual circumstances. I must admit that I was not there at the time of his death, and my information is based on what I heard later from friends, most of whom are now either themselves dead or sworn to secrecy. It appears that Arthur was accused of misconduct and cowardice in the face of the enemy; he faced some kind of military court. More than that I don't know, but I do know that Arthur was extremely, even recklessly, brave, and was a model officer. If there was any suspicion of misconduct I believe it was entirely unfounded. His CO at the time was Lt-Col Robbins, who died last year on the Somme …'

The rest of the letter held little of relevance, but in another letter from a Major Goodall (Rtd) dated January 1918 they found the following paragraph:

'As a fellow officer of the Regiment and a former colleague I must advise you not to pursue your quest for information any further. There will not be an official inquiry into the circumstances of your son's death even if you feel that you have the grounds for such an inquiry. Many things that we in the British Army cannot feel proud about have taken place in this ghastly War, and it will be years before the records can be put straight. I do advise you, my dear Reginald, to drop this matter now for your sake and for that of your wife.'

The final letters in the bundle were dated June 1918 and were condolences to Mrs Leaman on the death of her husband.

"We have to find out exactly what did happen."

"Oh no, Michael, let's leave the whole affair alone. Put the letters back in the shelves and board them up again."

"You really think that we can just walk away from this. Can't you see that we are destined to find out the truth: The medallion, the photograph, the letters. These are not coincidences; they are deliberate instructions!"

"Instructions! Instructions from whom?"

"I don't know, but I am convinced that unless we try to establish exactly what did happen on 29 March 1915, Leaman will not leave us in peace."

During the following months, Michael obsessionally researched the circumstances of Leaman's death, spending every spare moment and even his company's time and resources to establish the truth. At first the results were meagre: His death certificate recorded 'Died in action' and made no reference to a firing squad, and it was only by chance that he came across a brief reference to a court martial of two soldiers of the Royal Wiltshire Fusiliers which took place on 28 March 1915, the day before Leaman died.

Further enquiries to the Commonwealth War Graves Commission revealed that two privates in the Wiltshires, who had been executed by firing squad, lay buried in the British Cemetery at Petit Beaucourt: John Alfred Harbutt and James Archibald Sinclair. Using these names, Michael was then able to find, with the help of the Imperial War Museum, a brief account of the court martial. It appeared that during an attack on German positions on 15 March 1915, the two privates were discovered by field police in the jump-off trench some 90 minutes after the attack began. There was also a reference to an officer whose case would be heard separately.

Armed with this information, Michael now believed that he had found out all he could about Leaman, as he explained to his wife.

"Leaman was certainly the officer involved in the case, but because his father had been a major in the same regiment, he was given a separate court martial and his execution was kept secret. To all intents and purposes he fell in battle, and it was only through his personal contacts within the regiment that Major Leaman was able to discover that his son had been found guilty of cowardice."

"It must have been a terrible blow to him."

"It killed him."

"Despite the fact that fellow officers vouched for his son's bravery."

"Yes. His parents never knew what actually happened, no more than we can."

"So at last, we can let the whole affair rest. I must say, Michael, that there have been moments over the last 18 months when I wondered whether you had lost all your sense of the rational."

"That's a long winded way of saying that you thought I was going mad."

They both laughed and opened a bottle of wine to celebrate the end of the quest for Leaman.

It was barely a week later that the phone calls in Michael's office began.

"You have to know that I was totally innocent."

"Innocent of what? I don't understand. Linda, who is this on the line?"

"There is no one on the line, Mr Prescott."

"Well, I certainly heard someone. Please do not put through any calls without asking me first."

"I always check with you first, Mr Prescott. Surely you know that. There is no one on the line and I haven't put through a call." Linda added with more than a trace of anger in her voice.

A similar exchange took place two days later but again no call had come through the switchboard.

It was only after several of these exchanges that Michael realised that he was talking to Leaman.

"It's nothing to do with me. It all happened years ago and I'm no longer involved."

"Oh yes you are! I am going to tell you the truth and you will listen."

"That's where you're wrong. I have washed my hands of the whole affair," Michael replied replacing the receiver. "Linda, I suppose that you haven't put any calls through recently?"

"No, Mr Prescott, not since the call from Sun Alliance."

"I'm going mad, you know. I've just had a conversation with a man who died in 1915."

While it was easy to make a joke with the company's receptionist, it was much more difficult to put the conversation out of his mind. Over the next few days, Michael found concentrating on his work very difficult and came to dread the ringing of the phone. His work was keeping him in the London office and he was commuting by train from Newbury to Paddington each day. One evening as the packed commuter train slowed down in a tunnel, Michael who, along with many other office workers, was forced to stand, noticed the tall figure of a young man in military uniform pushing his way through the carriage towards him. At first he thought nothing of it and continued to read his newspaper despite the jostling of his fellow travellers, but as the figure got closer he recognised the lean features of Leaman. His mouth went dry and he felt a tremble begin in his leaden legs.

"Go away! I've told you I will have nothing more to do with you!"

The other passengers turned towards Michael in surprise.

"Sorry mate did you say something?"

"Stop haunting me. Get away! Get away!"

"Are you alright?" A kindly lady enquired. "It's a bit hot in here. Open the window someone, this gent's having a turn."

At that moment the train began to move out of the tunnel and, as daylight flooded back into the carriage, the figure of Leaman appeared to melt away.

"Didn't you see him?"

"Who?"

"That soldier."

"A soldier in uniform? You must be joking, mate. What with the IRA we don't see no uniforms these days, especially in trains."

"Overworking, dear," said the kindly lady. "A combination of overworking and the heat. My advice to you is to go sick for a few days."

Michael felt that his descriptions of these events to Jane were meeting with increasing hostility. Eventually in bed that evening, having listened in silence to Michael's account of what happened in the train, she stated her case in no uncertain terms.

"Look Michael, this obsession is driving me mad. Every moment we are together you talk about that damned soldier, at breakfast, lunch and dinner. We lie awake at night, not making love like normal couples, but speculating about what happened to Lt Leaman. Quite frankly I've had more than enough and so have the children. If you want to be married to Leaman, then tell us, and we can leave you and start again, but if you want to remain married to me, I never want to hear his name again. Do you understand? Really?"

"I want to be free of him as much as you do, but he keeps on pursuing me."

"For heaven's sake, take a grip on yourself. How can a soldier who died eighty years ago pursue an economics graduate from Manchester University, a successful manager, a rational, or so we are told, product of modern education? If it weren't so painful, I would find it quite laughable. A man with whom you have no family connections, no links, no physical or intellectual contact, a dead soldier from the Great War – how can this, this 'thing', this nonsense wreck our marriage and our lives? How? Tell me how?"

"I can't explain."

"Well, I am beginning to think that I can."

"What's that supposed to mean?"

"Well, I've never actually seen this figure …"

"You've heard his footsteps."

"It could have been the children, or a radio next door, anything. The only person who claims to have seen him is yourself, and quite frankly, I'm beginning to doubt your sanity."

"So you think I'm going mad?"

"I'm not the only one. Your assistant from work, Martin Jones …"

"Johnson. Martin Johnson."

"He spoke to me on the phone expressing his concern over your obsession."

"Did he now, well he should mind his own business."

"He reckoned you should spend more time minding the company's business."

"Did he indeed. Well good night."

In order to avoid the train, Michael drove the car the next morning as far as Turnham Green and took the tube to work. After the previous day's encounter, he felt very nervous and buried himself in the 'Financial Times' trying not to look around the carriage nor catch the eyes of his fellow passengers. At Hammersmith he changed onto the Piccadilly

Line to continue his trip to the West End where he had his first appointment of the day. The carriage was very crowded and he was forced to stand near the door; there was no room to read his paper so he fixed his gaze upon an advertisement for holidays in Cyprus. Then, reflected in the glass of the window, he saw it, a hideous and pitiful sight. Leaman, blood seeping from bullet wounds in his face and torso, his uniform in tatters, was pushing through the carriage towards him.

"No! No! Keep away from me! Stop haunting me; I know that you don't exist!" Michael shouted in terror, frightening the other passengers who stood back from him.

"Keep him away from me! Catch him!"

"Who are you talking about?" asked one passenger.

"He's hallucinating, poor chap," said another.

The mangled and bloody face of Leaman was now pressed close to Michael's who was clawing at the door of the train which had slowed down to a crawl outside Green Park Station. He could smell the putrefaction of death as Leaman pushed his mangled face closer and closer to his own.

"They killed me, the bastard British Army! Not the Germans. It broke my father's heart when he found out what they had done to me."

"Keep away from me! I don't want to know."

"Listen to me because I am going to tell you the truth whether you like it or not. The battalion was sent forward to launch an attack on the German positions outside Bethune and our company's objective was a trench opposite Oak Trench which the Germans were defending quite lightly. The attack was a complete success and we took the trench with few casualties. There were two new recruits, Harbutt and Sinclair who were really windy and had not come over with us. We suspected that they were hiding in the jump-off trench. Fatal that was in those days, as the Field Police would come around and either arrest them or shoot them on the spot as deserters. I volunteered to go back and bring them forward as it was quiet at the time. So I went back leaving the Captain and about 25 men in the German trench. I found the recruits alright, but after I had talked to them for a while and got them to agree to come over, the German's launched a fierce counter-attack. We were cut off in Oak Trench and it was then that the Field police came up. At first I felt confident that the captain would be able to clear up the situation and that the two recruits would get off, but when a few stragglers came back from the other side, saying that the Germans had recaptured the trench and either killed or taken all our men prisoner, I began to realise that I was in a difficult position. We were arrested and although I gave a clear account of what had happened, no one could corroborate my story. The Colonel was furious that the attack had failed, and was himself under threat of being Stellenbosched, or sent back to England, so he made an example of us three. The rest you know."

As Leaman was talking, Michael slowly slipped to the floor of the carriage his head in his hands, sobbing loudly and trying not to look at the bloody figure standing over him. The other passengers were alarmed, some believing that he was epileptic, others that he was having some kind of panic attack. As the train crept into Green Park station they decided to pull the alarm and call for medical help. Michael was removed from the train and taken by ambulance to Hammersmith Hospital where he was sedated and put under observation.

Awaking in a strange room, Michael at first had no idea where he was nor how he had got there, then some recollection of the previous day's events filtered into his conscience. He rang the bell by his bed and an attractive nurse with a sympathetic round face and honey blond hair cut into a bob came through the door.

"I must explain exactly what happened yesterday, and I must let my wife know where I am and my office too."

"It's all been done." The nurse replied smiling kindly. "Your wife is coming here this morning and your office is not expecting you for at least a week. You've had a bad experience and we must find out what has brought it on."

"That's easy to explain. Leaman, the soldier who has been haunting me … I know it sounds ridiculous, but I can explain it all. I know you think I'm hallucinating, but I have been pursued by Leaman."

"You must explain all this to the doctor when he comes."

"Doctor? I don't want to see a doctor. I must get out of here. Can't you understand that I'm perfectly alright. If it weren't for Leaman everything would be fine."

Michael got out of bed and looked around the room for his clothes.

"That's a clever trick, removing my clothes so I can't leave. But you must understand that there is nothing wrong with me. I should never have become involved with Leaman in the first place; it's all my fault I know, but I am determined now to be rid of the whole thing. I'm going home to throw away the letters and anything to do with the accursed man. If necessary, we'll move house to be rid of him once and for all. Please let me have my clothes back. I want to go home and sort everything out."

"I'll let you have your clothes back provided you promise to stay with me and do exactly what I say."

The nurse returned with his clothes and agreed to accompany Michael to his car at Turnham Green. They slipped out of the hospital with no hindrance and were soon driving out of London towards the M4.

"Why do you want to go straight home?" the nurse asked "Surely your house has too many associations? Why don't we take a few days' holiday together?"

"How could I possibly do that?" Michael exclaimed looking shocked.

"But you promised that you would do anything I said. If you don't co-operate I shall be forced to take you back to the hospital."

"I can't go back! Maybe I could take a few days off, but where shall we go."

"Head towards Dover. I suggest a few days in France together; it would be lovely," she added stroking Michael's leg. "I'm sure that your love life has been terribly interrupted by all your problems and maybe a few days together would help to sort them out. Think of it as a kind of therapy."

They bought two ferry tickets at Dover, and as they went through the ticket control, the official asked where the second passenger was.

"In the car right here of course!" Michael replied with some anger.

"As you say, sir," the official shrugged as he handed out the windscreen sticker.

From Calais they took the motorway south as the light began to fail.

"I know of a marvellous hotel in Bethune."

"No, darling, please I want to keep away from Bethune. Let's go further south; I don't mind driving all through the night. We could go to Burgundy."

"I really want to go back to this hotel in Bethune. I stayed there years ago and I have fond memories of it."

"Darling, please ..." Michael protested in vain as the nurse caressed his leg. "Alright we'll go there for the night, but we'll set off first thing in the morning for Burgundy."

The hotel, which was a small red brick building typical of late nineteenth century architecture in Northern France, was called 'Hotel de la Paix' and having been renamed after the Armistice in 1918. The owner stood behind the desk and without looking up grunted, "A single for one night?"

"Do you want a single, darling?" Michael asked the nurse.

"No, let's share tonight."

"Who are you talking to? A single?" the owner asked gruffly.

"No, we want a double."

The owner looked up briefly. "We? Oh well, as you wish."

They ate in the small cream-painted dining room which served as a watering hole for passing commercial travellers. The waitress seemed surprised that he wanted two meals, but commented jokingly that monsieur must be hungry.

After what was a surprisingly good meal, they retired to bed where they made love passionately, Michael realising just how much the Leaman affair had damaged his sexual appetite and the relationship with his wife. He swore to himself that on his return he would make amends and take Jane away for a second honeymoon.

The following morning, they set off early, driving out of Bethune towards the motorway, but just before they reached it, the nurse told Michael to pull into a turning on the left. At first Michael was unconcerned, but then he saw a familiar sight, the British Cemetery of Petit Beaucourt in the distance. It looked grim and fortress-like against the dark wood behind and a leaden grey sky.

"No! I'm never going back there!"

"Let's leave the car and walk across the field. I need a walk in the morning, and I certainly cannot sit for hours in the car without stretching my legs first."

"But not here, please."

The nurse got out of the car and began to walk across the field. She turned around beckoning to Michael. "If you really love me, you will come with me. I can show you something you've always wanted to see!"

As if in a trance Michael followed her across the field, through a fence and up the embankment which led to the motorway. The noise of the traffic was so great that it sounded to Michael like the roar of artillery. The nurse walked ahead still beckoning Michael onwards towards the road.

"Watch out, it's a busy road. We'll never be able to cross it here," Michael shouted above the noise.

The nurse calmly walked onto the motorway. "You love me, so come with me."

Controlling his fear, Michael stepped into the road. The nurse had disappeared and instead he saw a firing squad lined up facing their victim who was bound to a post. An officer was reading. "Lt Arthur Edward Leaman, Royal Wiltshire Fusiliers No 1956826. In accordance with the sentence of the court martial of 28 March you …"

Michael ran in front of the squad. “No, stop! He is innocent, he returned to the trench to bring the two new recruits across. He risked his life to save them. l know he is innocent …”

“Fire!”

The ‘Daily Telegraph’ the following day carried a short article:

‘The Minister of Health has ordered an enquiry into security at Hammersmith Hospital following the tragic death of Michael Prescott who absconded on Tuesday while under sedation. Prescott, aged 45 and father of three, was admitted for observation following an incident on the Underground. His disappearance was not reported for several hours, giving him time to take his car across the Channel. He apparently parked his car in a field near Bethune and wandered onto the motorway where he was struck by an oil tanker. He was killed instantly. French police could offer no explanation for the accident.’

# South of Kusadasi

The early morning April sun was shining as MTS Apollo docked at the only jetty at Kusadasi, a small but colourful Turkish seaside town whose main attraction is its closeness to the classical excavations at Ephesus. A few early risers were on deck as the cruise ship glided towards the jetty where a couple of Turks were waiting to take the warps and make her fast. To the south, across a little bay, the small Crusader fort glinted in the sun, while straight ahead the few passengers on the observation deck could see the exquisite fourteenth century caravanserai, its crenulations and stonework perfectly preserved in the pure air and dry climate of the Eastern Mediterranean. They could also see the tourist coaches arriving to take them to Ephesus once they had finished their English breakfasts in the dining room. On the open bridge below the observation deck the Greek captain was issuing orders through a mobile telephone while on the foredeck the deck hands were preparing to lower the anchor.

For Nigel and Jennifer, it had been a full and fascinating week. MTS Apollo had sailed from Athens calling at a number of Greek islands including Rhodes, Crete and Kos and they were now making their first visit to Turkey, before setting off the following day towards Cyprus where the cruise would end. They were pleased with their cabin, which was one of only a few to have a double bed and a proper bathroom, as opposed to a cramped shower-room. Most days had been spent sight-seeing and they were surprised at how much had been packed into such a short time. The evenings on board the ship had been slightly less successful at least at first. Many of the other passengers were elderly and had little interest in dancing or the nightly cabaret; moreover, conversation at dinner had sometimes been difficult. Nigel and Jennifer both worked in the City, had no children and no interest in gardening, television or the other pursuits of retired people. Consequently, they had suffered at least two evenings of boredom at the dinner table, having been seated without regard to interests, age or occupation.

The situation changed on the island of Rhodes, when they found themselves at lunch in a little taverna seated next to a young couple who also, it appeared, belonged to the cruise. They were an attractive pair; Richard was tall, dark haired and sun tanned, probably aged around 35, and Miranda, a willowy elegant blond, revealed her county background and Rodean School education in every gesture and sentence. They spent freely both on board and in the local restaurants, and it was quite natural that they should ask Nigel and Jennifer if they could join them at their table in the dining room.

As MTS Apollo edged its way out of Rhodes harbour one evening against an exquisite sunset of pinks, cerulean and viridian, the two couples met in the bar before going to the second sitting in the dining room. Their conversation was animated and Nigel and Jennifer felt that at last they had met some kindred spirits on the vessel. After dinner they viewed the cabaret together before retiring to the discotheque where they danced as a foursome until closing time at three o'clock in the morning, arranging before they went to bed, to meet on the coach the following day in Crete.

Both Nigel and Jennifer were sad when neither of their friends appeared on the coaches in the morning, and Nigel was inclined to return to the ship to see if they had overslept. However, knowing neither their surnames nor their cabin number, this was not feasible. Their surprise was great when they met their friends in the excavation at Knossos.

"We looked for you this morning, and we thought you had overslept."

"We were rather late, but we just managed to catch the second bus before it left," was Richard's explanation, which left Nigel slightly puzzled, as he had been quite sure that neither had been on the second coach as it left Heraklion.

That evening they again enjoyed a lively dinner together, the conversation turning to their respective jobs and homes in London, but neither Richard nor Miranda would be drawn into giving precise details. After the discotheque closed, Nigel and Jennifer strolled around the upper deck to get some fresh air, but as the ship was sailing fast, Jennifer soon began to feel the cold, so they went inside by a door towards the bows. As they walked the length of the boat to return to their cabin aft, they saw their friends entering a cabin on A deck, and as they passed they noticed the number A 58.

"I find them both quite reserved." Jennifer remarked to Nigel as they prepared for bed.

"They certainly play their cards close to their chests," Nigel added, "but I suspect it's a case of being modest about their possessions and position. I'm sure that Miranda comes from a very wealthy family."

"We still don't know their surnames."

"Maybe they're having a clandestine affair!"

"I hadn't thought of that, but it certainly explains everything. Yes, I'm sure you're right, they're both married, but not to each other."

The following evening was the Captain's Dinner and Nigel and Jennifer waited in the bar to have drinks with their friends before dinner, but neither appeared, and they found themselves eating alone on their table.

"Maybe one of them is ill," Jennifer suggested.

"Possibly, or else they've decided to eat in their cabin together."

"Oh you really think they can't bear our company!" Jennifer laughed.

"We can always pay them a visit after dinner. We know their cabin number, even if we don't know their surnames."

When the Captain had given a speech welcoming the passengers to MTS Apollo and when various toasts had been drunk, Nigel and Jennifer went to find their friends' cabin. However, as they walked along the starboard corridor on A deck they found that the last cabin before the bow was A 56; and as they cut across to the port side they found that all the cabins had odd numbers.

"I could have sworn that their cabin was on the starboard side."

"Maybe we're on the wrong deck."

"That's impossible, as they were entering a cabin on our deck, which is A."

"I'll go and ask reception for A58," Nigel said determined to clear up the confusion.

“There is no A58, sir,” the officer at the reception desk said without hesitation.

“In fact there is no cabin with a number higher than 56, and that is only on A deck. All the other decks have lower numbers. But take this photocopy of the deck plan; I’m sure you’ll find your friends. What is their name? I can look them up in the passenger list if you like, and give you their extension number.”

Nigel thanked the officer for his trouble, saying that he did not know their names, but that with the help of the plan he could locate their cabin. Together they retraced their steps of the previous evening, entering the door onto A deck and trying to locate the cabin. They knocked on the door that seemed closest in location, only to find a puzzled elderly couple preparing for bed, while the equivalent cabin on the port side yielded an irate lady from Rochdale who told them that they had no business knocking on cabin doors at this late hour of eleven o’clock.

Kusadasi was the last organised excursion ashore, as the following day would be spent at sea, before flying back from Cyprus. Ephesus proved to be a fascinating experience and both Nigel and Jennifer were amazed by the size of the ancient city and the quality of its architecture. After a lunch on board the Apollo, they wandered around Kusadasi entering the courtyard of the caravanserai where carpets were being made and sold. In the shadows they noticed Richard and Miranda deep in conversation with one of the carpet sellers. Waving over to them, they continued their walk around the town, but bumped into them again taking coffee near the main mosque.

“We missed you last night.”

"Miranda was very tired so we decided to eat in our cabin."

"You missed the highlight of the cruise – the Captain's Dinner," Jennifer added with just a trace of cynicism.

"Yes, tragically, but there we are."

"We tried to find your cabin, but …"

"Would you care for a coffee; this Turkish coffee is the best in the world you know. It was the Turks who brought coffee to Europe in the seventeenth century, it is said, during the siege of Vienna."

The rest of the afternoon was pleasantly spent together exploring the town and its Crusader fort, and, returning to the Apollo shortly before it sailed, they agreed to meet for drinks before dinner. As the sun fell towards the misty blue horizon, the ship slipped its mooring and headed south towards Cyprus, passing through the narrow straights which separate the Turkish mainland from the island of Samos. It was a moment of great beauty; on the left the mountain peaks of Turkey catching the setting sun; on the right the hills of Samos bathed in the pale blue shadows of an Aegean evening. As the Apollo cleared the straights and gained speed, the two couples went to the dining room to enjoy a special Greek evening during which they drank generous amounts of retsina to accompany a good meze. After dinner, they watched a spectacle of Greek dancing in the ship's lounge, but before midnight Miranda and Richard took their leave.

Jennifer suggested a stroll around the decks to clear their heads before going to bed, and together they circuited the boat on all three decks without seeing anybody, before finding themselves on the high sundeck at the stern. They watched the wash of the propellers disappearing into the distance and talked about the success of the cruise while hearing the faint sound of 'Zorba the Greek' coming from the lounge. Then they heard angry voices from a lower deck at the stern, and craning their necks over the railing, they saw Miranda and Richard arguing three decks below.

"Maybe we should stop them," Jennifer suggested.

"No, it's their affair and none of our business."

But as Nigel spoke, the argument developed into a violent fight. They could clearly see Richard forcing Miranda against the rails and punching her face.

"Hey, you two stop!" Nigel called out against the noise of the wind and the engines, but apparently he was not heard.

"We must go down and stop them. He's attacking her!"

To go down to the lower decks, they had to go forward and down steps at the side of the ship, and reluctant to take their eyes off the events taking place below, they remained rooted to the spot. Richard had now got Miranda in a neck lock and was lifting her up as if trying to throw her overboard.

"My God!" cried Jennifer. "He's trying to drown her. Nigel you must stop them."

As Nigel ran towards the steps, Jennifer followed the fight, and within a few instants of Nigel's departure, she saw the struggling body of Miranda disappearing into the white foam of the propellers. For a few minutes she saw her head black against the foam, but as the light from the ship faded, and as the foam dispersed, Miranda disappeared from sight.

Jennifer joined Nigel as he ran down the three flights of steps, but as they arrived on the lowest aft deck, they saw no one.

"Raise the alarm; stop the ship!" Nigel was already inside running along the corridor towards the officer on duty at the reception desk. "Raise the alarm," he repeated over and over again. "Someone has been thrown overboard. We've seen it with our own eyes."

As the Apollo slowed down and began a wide circling of the area, all the guests were called to their muster stations to be checked off against the passenger list, a process which took some time and caused great anger not only from those who had already gone to bed but also from those dragged away from the Greek dancing. By 1:30 am all the passengers had been checked and none found missing; the Apollo completed a last circle before resuming its southward passage towards Limassol.

"God, what a fool I feel!" Jennifer said bitterly once they had returned to their cabin.

"Did we really see a murder? Were we imagining it, or were those two acting out some sort of drama in order to fool us?"

"It didn't look like acting to me. Richard really appeared to be punching Miranda in a most violent way. I was going down the stairs when you saw the woman going overboard, so you are the only witness to that, but we both saw the fight. I just can't believe they were acting."

"I definitely saw Miranda in the water; I could see her quite clearly in the light from the boat, and yet they say no passengers are missing. Mark you, they weren't around when the staff were checking the passenger list."

"No, but that doesn't mean anything. There are three muster stations on board," Nigel said looking at the notice on the cabin door. "They would have been in the lounge as their cabin is forward."

"We don't know where their cabin is; it could be anywhere. I feel such a fool. How am I going to show my face in the dining room again?"

"Nobody knows that it was us who raised the alarm."

"False alarm," Jennifer said bitterly.

"No, we were right to raise the alarm; I just can't understand what's happened."

There was a knock at the door and the ship's purser came in.

"I feel such a fool …" Jennifer started.

"No you mustn't, madam," the purser replied. "You did the right thing raising the alarm, and I can assure you it has happened before."

"Not a false alarm, surely."

"I am not at liberty to say anything further. All I can ask you to do is not to discuss the matter with anyone on the ship nor on your return home. We plan to inform all the passengers in the morning that this was a practice emergency which under Greek maritime law we have to carry out twice a year."

After the purser had left, they discussed the night's events until dawn began to break. They both agreed that the purser knew more than he was prepared to admit and that he was saddened rather than angered by the false alarm. Luckily the following day was to be spent at sea, and both Nigel and Jennifer were able to make up their lost sleep dozing on deck in the strong spring sunshine.

That evening, the last of the cruise, they decided to join another table for dinner, not wanting to eat alone and being apprehensive about meeting their friends, whose absence on board during the day at sea had been noticeable. As they sat down to join an elderly couple on a table for six, Miranda and

Richard joined them. Jennifer hands began to tremble uncontrollably and she dropped a fork onto her plate, also overturning a full wine glass. The conversation quickly turned to the previous night's alarm.

"They told us it was a practice alarm," the elderly man said. "If so, it was damned inconvenient. We were both asleep, and the alarm bells really shook us."

"It can give older people heart attacks, that kind of excitement," his wife added.

"Where were you two?" Nigel asked turning towards Richard and Miranda.

"Oh, we had just got to sleep when the chaos began. I wanted to stay in bed, but Miranda said that if anyone was missing they would check all the cabins."

"You weren't on the aft deck were you?" Nigel continued.

"No, why do you ask?"

"I saw you there," Jennifer said loudly, "both of you, having a fight."

"It was a fright," said the elderly lady, "and it ruined the Greek evening for us."

Richard took this opportunity to change the subject. "I hope this won't delay our arrival in Limassol. What time is the flight?"

Neither couple wanted to extend the evening; Miranda and Richard refused pudding, made excuses about having to pack their suitcases and left the table.

"I think we should have a walk on deck."

"Absolutely not. I refuse."

"Yes, but we must get it out of our system." Nigel persisted. "Let's go and stand in the same place on the aft deck and rid ourselves of the vision, if that's what it was."

They stood in the same place as the previous night, talking over the events and trying to find a rational solution which would satisfy their rational minds. After nearly an hour's talking they returned to their cabin.

"It's very cold in here," Nigel commented adjusting the air conditioning.

"And there's a slight smell of cigarette smoke. I suppose it has seeped under the door."

As Jennifer went to the bathroom to remove her makeup, Nigel heard a terrifying scream, and racing in he saw the bloated body of Miranda floating in the bath which was full of cold, dirty water. Her face was bruised and swollen, the flesh slimy and turning green. One eye was open, the other had been eaten by a fish leaving a lifeless black socket. Her lips had also been eaten revealing her perfect white teeth which appeared to be smiling hideously at the ceiling. Her body was almost naked, except for some fragments of clothing and strands of dark green seaweed; the skin was still white, but areas of bruising had turned a livid purple with blackening edges. The only remnant of her former beauty was her golden hair which floated around her ravaged face like a Pre-Raphaelite painting of the drowning Ophelia. Jennifer was on the floor gasping for breath and retching.

Nigel ran to call the duty officer, but on their return found the bath empty, shining clean and quite dry.

"I simply cannot explain this," he mumbled to the officer. "I am going mad, it was there without any doubt – a hideous corpse, which we both saw." Jennifer had recovered a little and was sitting on the edge of the bath sobbing gently. "Half of me is frightened, but the other half is angry," he said, his voice rising. “There is something that you know about which you’re not telling us.”

They were joined in the cabin by the purser and the English cruise organiser who invited them to sit quietly and have a drink which he ordered from the steward.

“There is something that you ought to know, and which I suppose we should have told you last night. You are not the first couple to have been disturbed in this way, and sadly probably not the last.”

“What on earth is that supposed to mean?” Nigel asked aggressively his fear quickly turning to fury.

“Just what I say. Other couples have seen exactly the same vision of a young pair fighting on the aft deck and the man throwing the woman overboard. It all started about two years ago when a man called Richard Farmer ‘lost’ his wife on the last night of a cruise. They had been at the Greek evening, and he said that his wife wanted to go for a walk around the deck to clear her head, but he, having had too much to drink, went to his cabin and fell asleep, or so he claimed. When he awoke in the morning, his wife was not with him and he raised the alarm. Of course, she could have been overboard for up to seven hours and would have been miles away. We did a thorough search, but she was never found, nor was her body. This part of the Mediterranean is very deserted so she had no chance of being spotted by a passing boat.”

“What was her name?” Jennifer asked, already knowing the answer.

“Miranda. She came from a wealthy family and there was the suspicion that her husband had killed her to get her inheritance, but there was no proof.”

“What happened to him?”

"The Greek police were very suspicious, and were convinced that he had murdered her, but there was not a shred of evidence. No one had seen her on deck; no one had seen any sign of a struggle or even of an argument over dinner; there were no blood stains or signs of violence. You know yourselves how deserted the decks become after dark, and there were simply no witnesses. She just disappeared off the face of the earth. The Greek police held Richard Farmer in a prison in Athens for several months, but they had to release him for lack of evidence."

"But we know he murdered her," Jennifer said.

"Several people have seen what looks like a murder taking place, but this is hardly concrete evidence. The couple you saw simply did not exist; they had no cabin, they were not on the passenger list, they were never on board."

"But they ate at our table, there must be witnesses, both passengers and staff, who can testify that they existed."

"Of course they were seen, but they do not exist. They have been seen on three cruises since the event and always on the last two nights; they befriend couples of their own age and … well, you know the rest of the story. We have tried to exorcise the ship and we intend on changing its name, but whether this will have any effect is impossible to say. It's very bad for the crew and the passengers; when the alarm is raised we have to stop and carry out a search, but know nothing will be found. We have warned the crew to look out for them, but each time they appear they look slightly different and cannot be distinguished from the rest of the passengers. All we can do is apologise and beg you not to tell anybody back in England about it, or else the cruise company, and even the Apollo will be bankrupt."

Four months later Nigel and Jennifer were walking down Bond Street having been to the Royal Academy Summer Exhibition. As they passed the windows of Aspreys, they were accosted by a well-dressed young couple.

"Dear God, it's Richard and Miranda!" Jennifer shrieked.

"Marvellous to see you both," Richard said in his urbane manner apparently quite unaware of Jennifer's extreme anxiety. "Can I introduce you to Miranda's twin sister, Sabrina?"

# A Split-Second Decision

Occasionally you come across a couple who seem perfect in every way – in looks, in academic and financial success, in marriage, in life. Alastair and Melanie Stuart were just such a couple living a perfect life in the perfect city of Bath. Alastair was a successful heart surgeon at the Royal United Hospital in Bath but also held a lecturing post at Bath Spa University while his wife Melanie was a solicitor specialising in international law who was often in London or abroad. Despite their high powered lives both seemed relaxed and unstressed. They sometimes entertained in their late Georgian house just off Widcombe Hill and their friends were impressed by the cool elegance of the house with its views over Bath.

Behind Alastair's façade of cool authority and competence lay a difficult past. He had been born in a rundown house in Comely Bank in Edinburgh. His parents were relatively old when Alastair was born and as an only child he was the apple of his mother's eye. She protected him, pushed him academically at school and seemed determined to invest in him the success which had eluded her and her husband. Not that Alastair's father was a failure: far from it, as he had risen to become a local bank manager, but had been forced into early retirement when his branch was closed. The option of taking a step backward in status working in another branch appealed even less than early retirement, but there had been no realistic alternative. Still, with his interest in golf and cycling, early retirement had its attractions. Mr Stuart had always enjoyed a dram of whisky and a pint in the pub after work, but with retirement the opportunities of drinking expanded and he no longer had to worry about appearances in the office. Slowly, but surely, drinking became an integral part of his life. A few beers in the club after a round of golf with friends might be the prelude to a visit to the pub in Stockbridge on the way home: A cycle ride with friends would often lead to an alcoholic lunch in a country pub. Slowly but surely alcohol became a central part of Mr Stuart's life and at time, frustrated with his lack of position in society and slightly inebriated, he would vent his anger on his only son, Alastair. He would accuse him of indolence, of lack of sporting prowess, of being a mother's boy. In fact, he would accuse him of anything that sprung to mind.

Alastair understood his father's problems and found that the best way to cope was to avoid him. He worked very hard on his school studies especially when he embarked on three scientific 'A' Levels – Chemistry, Biology and Physics with which he hoped to pass into Medical School. He attended after school classes as well as playing squash in the evenings and often at the weekends. Avoidance, he discovered, was a better tactic than confrontation, especially as his mother would always stand up for him against his father which often led to major family rows.

Alastair's own relationship with alcohol was complicated. He hated seeing his father returning from the golf course or pub lit up and rather aggressive, but never actually drunk. As a young boy he had respected and admired his father setting off to the bank smartly dressed in a dark suit and tie with polished black shoes. This was his image of the past and he disliked seeing what he perceived to be a shocking decline in his father appearance and manner. Alastair blamed alcohol for his father's fall from grace and would refuse to partake when out with his friends. Yet one Saturday morning after several vigorous games of squash he joined his partner at a newly opened 'gastropub' in Edinburgh New Town. Refusing the usual pint, Alastair was tempted by his partner's girl friend who had joined them for lunch to order a glass of dry white sauvignon from New Zealand. The fresh taste of the wine with its hints of gooseberry and citrus struck Alastair as exquisite and much better than any beer that he had ever tasted. After a second glass, he noticed a feeling of contentment and well-being which he both enjoyed and feared. He realised that it would take very little for him to be as attracted to alcohol as his father and he knew that he would have to be extremely wary treading a path between abstinence and very controlled enjoyment of fine wines.

Helped by his mother's encouragement and belief, Alastair did well at 'A' Level and was offered a number of university places to study medicine. One Saturday morning a letter arrived with and offer to an interview at Gonville and Caius College, Cambridge. Alastair's father expressed his support but in a somewhat grudging manner and Alastair awaited an aggressive diatribe about moving up in the world from his father later that evening. His mother expressed delight at the offer and encouraged Alastair to attend, although he could see from her eyes that she dreaded living in Comely Bank without her son. To clear his head Alastair went for a long walk, up through Circus Place and Howe Street followed by a circuit along Princes Street and back through Queen Street. While walking it became obvious to Alastair that he simply could not leave his mother to suffer the increasingly unpleasant company of his father. He would have to attend University of Edinburgh Medical College and live at home.

Once accepting this disappointment, Alastair threw himself into his studies in Edinburgh and eventually qualified with top marks. After his first year he moved into a flat with some other medics, but returned regularly to Comely Bank where he managed to raise his mother's spirits and keep her busy with her many part time charity jobs in the city. He rarely spoke with his father, but was able to keep their relationship on an even keel.

After leaving University, Alastair had several hospital jobs which eventually led to an appointment as Consultant Cardiologist at Bath's Royal United Hospital. His father had died and his mother seemed happy in sheltered accommodation in Edinburgh, so Alastair took up his new appointment with a clear conscience, no longer tied to Comely Bank. Not long after taking up his new post he met Melanie at a dinner arranged by some friends. She had come from a very different background. The daughter of a senior civil servant she studied law at Bristol University and had worked her way up to becoming partner in an international law company. After a brief engagement they were married in Bath Abbey, Melanie's father having pulled some diplomatic strings.

To all observers, Alastair and Melanie made a golden couple. Alastair was tall and had dark good looks. He also spoke with an attractive Edinburgh accent which many found appealing. Melanie was also tall, elegant with shoulder length blond hair, a perfect English rose in every respect. But of course appearances can deceive and beneath the idyllic surfaces tensions were developing. The first issue was their inability to conceive despite special treatment over a period of time. Eventually they resigned themselves to being a childless couple and even made a virtue of it, allowing themselves regular trips abroad. Underneath the elegant façade, however, both regretted their inability to have a family.

Alastair's work at the hospital often demanded very long hours and sometimes he would sleep at the hospital after a long night's operation. Melanie was also deeply involved in her work. Her firm had its main office in London and Melanie would commute regularly to London by train, and quite often stay in a hotel overnight. She also worked abroad, particularly in Europe where she worked in conveyancing helping British investment trusts acquire commercial property in the European Union. Often the couple only met up at the weekend 'like ships passing in the night'. Alastair suspected Melanie of having affairs but strangely was not too concerned, feeling that an open marriage was probably better than resentment. He himself was popular with female staff at the hospital and when Melanie was abroad or in London he would invite female colleagues back to the house. These infidelities were unknown to friends and neighbours who considered them a perfect couple.

Life could probably have continued in this pleasant and fulfilling manner, but sometimes in life a decision taken in a split second that can change the course of the future for ever.

The modern concept of the revolving door is maybe the equivalent of the medieval belief in the wheel of fate: a coincidence of time and space which can lead to either joy or despair. Alastair's story is about an instant irreversible decision taken in seconds and regretted over decades.

Alastair and Melanie were invited to a Sunday lunch party with legal friends in the nearby village of Norton St Philip. The couple were both solicitors and Melanie had met them through her work. The party consisted of couples of their age mostly with children who enjoyed the fine summer weather in the large garden complete with swings and a paddling pool. Lunch started late and innumerable bottles of wine seemed to appear on the table. Melanie and Alastair tossed a coin to see who would drive home and Alastair was happy to remain sober as he was operating the following day. During the lunch Melanie was highly animated. Admired by the male guests she also seemed to attract the children around her.

As the lunch progressed Alastair felt more and more alienated from his wife, a feeling of loss above all. He consoled himself with a few glasses of cold white wine, but after the meal the party divided into groups sitting in different areas around the garden. Alastair found himself sitting next to a very attractive young woman who was a trainee solicitor recently out of university and working in their host's practice. His mind returned to the early years of his marriage to Melanie and he found himself flattered by his new acquaintance's attention. He began to realise that his marriage was failing, not due to rows or disputes, but just to indifference and lack of passion. As the wine flowed, Alastair felt his inhibitions and reservations evaporating, a pleasant feeling. As the sun declined the hosts suggested that they should all partake of a light supper to finish a perfect day and more wine slipped down. It was already dark when Melanie suggested that they should head for home, thanking Alastair for his sacrifice. Although he was almost certainly over the limit, Alastair felt himself perfectly capable of driving the short distance home.

Alastair knew the A36 well, which led down into Bath from Norton St Philip, from many years of driving in and around Bath. As the road known as the Warminster Road descends towards Midford Brook it has a steep embankment on the right where the ground falls sharply away through trees. It was usually a busy road and stopping or parking were strictly forbidden, however as Alastair took the sharp bend just beyond Monkton Lodge, he saw a large van parked without lights. Alastair pulled out sharply to avoid the illegally parked van, clipped it with his front wing and wheel which threw the car to the right, across the road, over the low wall and down the steep incline.

His prevalent memory of the next moments was shocking noise: the noise of the car hitting trees and turning onto its roof and back again, Melanie's piercing cries of horror and pain, the noise of the windscreen shattering. And then silence. Total silence; no police sirens, no emergency services, no drivers of other cars.

Alastair regained consciousness for a few moments. It was pitch black outside and he realised that nobody had seen the accident. He looked at Melanie who was still strapped to her seat beside him. She was obviously in a very bad way. A thick branch had come through the window and was embedded in her chest. Her face was severely lacerated by glass from the windscreen and she was completely covered in blood. Alastair's initial reaction as a doctor was that she was dead, but he felt a pulse. For a few seconds his mind raced. If he called emergency services now on his phone which he could feel in his pocket, the police would certainly breathalyse him and find him over the limit. His career would be ruined and he would probably face a gaol sentence. In his view the emergency services might not be able to save Melanie but if he waited until dawn he might well avoid gaol and Melanie would still have a chance to live. These thoughts lasted a few seconds before he fell back into unconsciousness.

When Alastair finally awoke, the sun was shining in his face through the shattered windscreen. Still silence apart from the morning chorus of birds and the distant sound of traffic. He reached for his phone, but felt a searing pain in his hand and realised that his wrist was broken. With his other hand he withdrew his phone from his pocket but its screen was shattered and was useless. He managed to open the car door and scramble painfully up the embankment onto the A36. The morning rush hour was in full swing; the van had gone but the skid marks of the car were clearly visible. A passing motorist, horrified by Alastair's bloody appearance, stopped and offered to help, quickly calling the police and the emergency services.

Help arrived shortly, but Melanie was declared dead while Alastair was hospitalised. His injuries were limited to a broken wrist and a deep cut to his head which had been caused by the crushing of the car roof. While in hospital Alastair was visited by the police who wanted to know more about the accident and how much he had drunk at the party at Norton St Philip. Luckily for him, the police had discovered traces of dark green paint on the off side wing of the car which proved the presence of a parked van, although all attempts to trace the van had so far proved fruitless. Alastair realised that he was in danger of being prosecuted for dangerous driving while under the influence, but was also aware that the police would have difficulty in proving this.

The next weeks passed in something of a daze. His medical colleagues rallied around giving him moral and physical support, bringing food around, helping him with the funeral arrangements, attending the coroner's inquest with him and dealing with insurance and other legal matters. One colleague who worked with the police told him that he had had a lucky escape and that the police had seriously considered taking action against him, but were put off by lack of evidence. The worst day was Melanie's funeral but again he was supported by friends and colleagues, although Melanie's parents were coolly angry and seemed to hold Alastair responsible for the death of their daughter. Nevertheless, life did return to normal and after a period of convalescence Alastair returned to his work at the Royal United Hospital.

One evening, some four months after the accident, Alastair returned to the house off Widcombe Hill to prepare dinner for Jane, a theatre nurse in the cardiology department with whom he had been conducting in a casual relationship for some years. Since the accident their meetings had become more regular and frequent. Jane's own marriage had broken down some years before and her only daughter was away at university. Alastair unloaded the shopping he had picked up on the way back from work, and went to the telephone to pick up his messages. Since the accident he had received many messages from friends as well as work colleagues. He listened to the messages making notes on the pad he kept by the phone and deleting those he no longer needed.

Then, to his horror, came a simple message; 'You killed me' spoken clearly and precisely by Melanie. Alastair dropped the phone as if it were hot. He eventually picked up the receiver and replayed the messages, but it was gone. He was convinced that he had heard Melanie, but the doorbell rang and Jane appeared ready for supper and a night with the consultant she so admired. Alastair poured wine for Jane, but took a large whisky for himself which helped steady his nerves and soon the incident was forgotten, obliterated from his memory as the accident itself.

It was some months before another incident, once again just a passing instant. Alastair used Facebook to keep in touch with friends and colleagues who had moved to jobs in other parts of the country. One evening after work he received an email saying that he had five new messages. When he clicked on the email, a photograph appeared of Melanie as she had been in the car, her face covered in blood. A second image appeared showing her chest pierced by the branch with a simple caption; 'You killed me'. Standing up abruptly he shouted at the screen. "I didn't kill you!"

A new image appeared on the screen showing the wrecked car being taken away by the police but with the caption; 'But you could have saved me'. Unable to look at the screen, Alastair went into the kitchen and poured himself a large malt whisky. When he had recovered his composure he returned to the screen, but was unable to find any of the images. They had all been deleted. He was fairly convinced that the telephone recording and the Facebook messages were the work of Melanie's brother who worked in computing and social media. He decided to arrange a visit to Melanie's parents on the pretext of taking some of her favourite jewellery and photographs. The parents were certainly cool, but Alastair did not feel that they blamed him directly for Melanie's death nor did he believe that they had posted the Facebook images. He felt their sadness and regret rather than open hostility.

So far Alastair had avoided going over the events of that fateful Sunday, but as he drove back to Bath he began to consider the meaning of the messages. The human mind is capable of self-deception. A murderer can convince himself that he is innocent, a fraudster can believe that he acted in his client's best interest, and Alastair was aware of that split second instant when he decided not to call the emergency services, although he had put it entirely out of his mind. Had he really abandoned his wife to save his career? He convinced himself that he had not been fully conscious when he made the decision and was suffering concussion from his head injury. Convinced, as he was, of his innocence, he continued his work and social life, but doubts remained, and doubts can multiply.

He went over the events of that night, time and time again, keeping himself awake until dawn and dominating his thoughts during the day. He tried to obliterate these persistent doubts by attending social events and meeting friends but also by drinking more in the evenings, and he would regularly call in at a supermarket on his way back from work to buy scotch or wine. Then he began to catch glimpses of women who looked remarkably like Melanie, sometimes in the street or while shopping. Waiting for a train to London at the station, he was convinced he saw Melanie in a train coming in the opposite direction.

When Alastair heard that his mother had died in a Leith nursing home aged 98, he was sad but also rejoiced in his mother's long life. The funeral was a modest affair as most of her friends had long since died and her son was well established in the South. Alastair attended along with some cousins and more distant relations. There was no church service but a short ceremony was held at the crematorium in a modern chapel. As the service drew towards its conclusion, the curtains closed over the coffin and at that moment the figure of Melanie dressed in a black legal gown and wig, which she had used for rare court sessions, appeared on the stage drawing the curtains aside. He looked straight ahead, descended the steps and walked down the aisle towards Alastair. On reaching his seat, she seized his arm and hissed, "You killed me!"

"No!" Alastair shouted. "I did not. I did all I could to save you."

"But instead of calling an ambulance, you decided to wait until the morning for fear of losing your career. You know exactly what you did. You sacrificed me for your career."

"No! No! I couldn't call an ambulance because my phone was dead."

"But you didn't know that at the time. Don't try to deceive yourself, you killed me and you know it."

Alastair's cousin who was standing beside him put his arm around him to comfort him.

"I realise just how much you loved your mother and what sacrifices you made to keep her happy, but you must let her go."

"I didn't kill her! I did all I could to save her," Alastair replied with tears streaming down his face. His cousin gently guided him down the aisle towards the exit. "Of course you did. We all appreciate what you did for your mother."

"She's there! There! Over there!"

"There is no one there, Alastair."

His cousin drove Alastair to his house in Edinburgh where he calmed him and told that under no circumstances was he to drive home that day, not until he had recovered from his mother's death. Other members of the family came to comfort Alastair in his loss and after a good rest with family and friends around, Alastair finally left to drive home two days later.

Listening to classical music on the radio, Alastair managed to keep the events at the funeral out of his mind. His powerful Audi seemed to eat the miles and with the sun shining Alastair began to enjoy the drive home on the relatively uncrowded motorway. Driving at some speed in the fast lane, he became aware of a problem with the steering which seemed to be pulling him towards the left. He dragged the wheel to the right and the car swerved, causing the car behind to flash his lights. Shortly after steadying the car, Alastair saw a hand reaching over and dragging the wheel towards the left. This time Alastair could not correct the steering and the car moved into the middle lane very nearly hitting a van which was forced to pull into the fast lane. The driver hooted and gesticulated, but Alastair was busy trying to prise the hand off the steering wheel.

The Audi continued to lurch towards the left and it was by pure luck that it reached the slow lane without hitting a large articulated truck which was forced to brake suddenly. Seeing a lay by ahead, Alastair managed to pull in and stop the car.

The articulated lorry its hooter blaring passed within a few inches of the Audi.

He turned to the passenger seat where Melanie was sitting, her face no longer drenched in fresh blood, but covered in scabs and suppurating sores.

"You nearly killed me!" he shouted. "And you could have killed others."

"In that split second decision you sealed my fate in order to save your career. You know that. But I'm not going to kill you. No, it's your career I'm going to kill."

The relationship with Jane continued, although they were both careful not to make it public to friends or colleagues in the hospital. Jane would regularly spend the weekend with Alastair, and this friendship was a great comfort to Alastair who was trying to get on with his career and put the accident behind him. One morning after a night spent with Jane, Alastair went downstairs to make coffee and returned with a tray with freshly made filter coffee and two croissants. Instead of Jane relaxing in the bed, he saw Melanie, her nightgown stained dark brown with congealed blood. In horror he dropped the tray and pointed speechlessly at the figure.

"Don't think you have got rid of me so easily. I will follow you wherever you go. I will visit you whenever I want. I will make your life hell."

Jane had leapt out bed and run across trying to rescue the breakfast tray. Alastair was in deep shock standing repeating.

"How much longer must I take this? How much longer can I stand this?" he repeated.

Jane realised that this was a throwback to the accident and tried to get Alastair to talk it through over the following months. But Alastair was unable to explain the reasons for his visions. He simply could not admit to anyone that he might have been responsible for Melanie's death. He continued to see visions and eventually Jane found that continuing a relationship with a deeply disturbed man was impossible. One evening she booked a table at a French restaurant near the Theatre Royal which they both liked. She had decided that over dinner she would tell him that the relationship was at an end.

"I don't want to hurt you, and I even love you, but I simply cannot continue with this strange relationship. It's as if you are only here part time and you are never fully committed to me. We can remain friends and we will continue to be professional colleagues, but we cannot be lovers."

Before Alastair could reply, he realised that a third person had joined their table. Melanie was dressed in lime green, a colour that had always suited her blond hair, and she looked wonderful. She put her hand on his as if to express her understanding of his disappointment and loss, but said nothing.

Alastair's medical colleagues had begun to notice a difference in his performance. One nurse had reported that she thought he had attended a morning clinic while still under the influence of a previous night's drinking. At an important conference in London Alastair gave a very poor presentation. He was convinced that he could see Melanie amongst the delegates which disturbed his delivery and many felt that his personal tragedy was affecting his state of mind.

A senior manager approached him in the hospital to suggest, in the politest of terms, that he take some grief counselling. An appointment was set up which Alastair willingly attended and he went over the accident and his personal loss frankly and in detail. But he omitted to mention his decision to delay calling an ambulance. After several sessions, the counsellor was convinced that he was hiding something from him.

"There is something you are not telling me, something that is at the root of your disturbance."

"I have told you everything in great detail. There is nothing I can add," Alastair replied, and they mutually agreed to end the therapy sessions.

Alastair's colleagues were unhappy that he had ended the therapy sessions and continued to be concerned about his welfare. They noticed that his hands often shook during operations, whereas before he was well known for his steady hand and cool precision. Various members of staff had noticed him drinking in pubs and bars late into the night, and he began to look unshaven and unkempt, very different from the former immaculately dressed consultant they had known. His former lover Jane had maintained a professional relationship with him, but was acutely aware of his erratic and unpredictable behaviour.

The situation came to a head one day during a long and complicated operation. Alastair had begun to take himself in hand and had avoided pubs and bars for over a week prior to the operation. He had nearly completed the procedure when he noticed that Jane was unmasking.

"We're not finished yet, Jane," he said before realising that it was Melanie behind the mask. Her face was no longer covered in blood nor in scabs, but was crisscrossed by ugly and livid scars.

"But you are finished, Alastair. You will never perform another operation."

Alastair stared at the vision dropping his scalpel and shouting. "Leave me alone, leave me in peace. Get out of here – this is my domain."

His colleagues tried to calm Alastair down but he ran out of the operating theatre leaving an assistant to complete the operation. The following day he was called into his supervisor's office and received a written warning about his behaviour. He was also offered a year's sabbatical to recover from his personal loss, but Melanie had been right and Alastair never worked again as a consultant.

His sabbatical year stretched into two years, then three. He sold the house off Widcombe Hill and moved into a flat near the Canal where he still lives. He has a few friends that he meets in the pub, but they are not real friends, just drinking companions. Bored by day and frightened by night, Alastair wanders the streets of Bath. He talks to himself, argues with invisible visions, frightens children but is quite harmless. You might well meet him sitting by the canal or on a bench in Victoria Park, in summer often dressed in pyjamas under an old dressing gown, in winter in an Army surplus trench coat. He will tell you that he was once a heart surgeon, one of the best in the country. You won't believe him, of course, but spare a moment to listen to his story. He will tell you about a split second decision that had ruined his life. You will give him a coin and walk away, but remember … It could have been you.

# The Dream

When Paul Weiss was 18 he had a vivid dream, so vivid that it woke him up. He sat up in bed trembling and went into the bathroom to have a drink of water. Returning to bed, he hoped that the second part of the night would be more restful. But the dream returned, as if a second instalment. It was a dream he was never to forget.

He was flying from New York, where he lived, to Brussels but as the plane approached Brussels airport it was engulfed in fog. The pilot attempted to make a landing based entirely on radar, but found himself in the wrong position, too low and too far down the runway. He called to passengers to adopt the brace position as he tried to land on what remained of the runway, but at that moment, the moment of awakening, the plane crashed into buildings at the end of the runway. The second incarnation of Paul's dream repeated the tragedy in even more lurid details with fire lapping at Paul's face and hands. He awoke screaming in horror.

For years afterwards, every mention of Brussels reminded Paul of this dream. Working in international finance for a New York company he was obliged from time to time to travel to Brussels but he always managed to avoid direct flights, going via Amsterdam and on by train or taking the

Eurotunnel from London. One day, however, his boss called him into his office to tell him that he was to go to Brussels the following day.

"Your team leader has tested positive for Covid, so you have to take his place at the conference in Brussels. Pack a bag and be at John F Kennedy by eight tomorrow. Here are your tickets."

"I cannot fly to Brussels."

"Why's that?"

"I had this dream …"

"Come on, Paul, we all have dreams. The tickets are booked and we are counting on you to attend the conference. Once you're on the flight with your colleagues your superstitions will evaporate."

The flight from New York to Brussels was torture for Paul. He jumped at the slightest disturbance, started at any announcement from the cockpit, took sleeping pills to steady his nerves and repeatedly visited the toilets. He ordered several gin and tonics but refused anything to eat. He arrived safely in Brussels, although he was a physical and mental wreck.

The conference lasted several days, and Paul had begun to relax, feeling at last that he had conquered his superstitions.

*Dreams are dreams and have no roots in reality*, he reflected. *It's extraordinary that I have been obsessed by a dream that happened over ten years ago.*

The return flight was uneventful at first and Paul was relaxed enough to fall asleep. However mid-Atlantic pockets of disturbance began to shake the plane, getting worse as the plane approached land. Paul feared that he had misinterpreted his dream and that the crash had taken place returning from

Brussels not flying to Brussels. No amount of sleeping pills and gin and tonic could settle his nerves, but the pilot performed a perfect landing at JFK.

Paul returned to his New York office in Liberty Street where his boss debriefed him on the conference. Having finally conquered his fears he felt both elated and free. He phoned his girlfriend to suggest a lunch date which she readily accepted. The sun was shining, he had overcome his ridiculous superstition, he was meeting his girlfriend and was even thinking of proposing. He walked briskly down the street, dodged past a man walking slowly with the aid of a stick, moved left to avoid a woman with a pushchair and slipped on the kerb. His head hit a bus pulling into the bus stop. His demise was painless.

# The Maid

It was love at first sight. Neither Paul nor Diana had ever imagined that they would be able to afford such a beautiful example of early Georgian architecture situated within a few miles of their work in the City. Called Rainsborough House, possibly after a Parliamentary colonel of the Civil War, its London stock brick facade was set off by tall, elegantly detailed sash windows and a front door slightly recessed beneath a beautifully carved and columned porch. Possibly its closeness to two busy roads made it unsuitable for older people, for over the years Rainsborough House had changed hands a surprising number of times, but both Paul and Diana reckoned that with double glazing and a careful use of curtains, the intrusion of the traffic could be minimised. Maybe its crowning glory, that ingredient that ensured that it always sold quickly, were the views over London which, from near the top of Highgate Hill, were magnificent at all times of the day. The land behind the house fell away steeply and to get to the back garden, which lay some 15 feet below the back windows, you had to go out of the front door and negotiate some steep steps which lay to the side of the house. Another unusual feature was an underground passage, long since blocked, that went under Highgate Hill and reputedly emerged in the basement of Lauderdale House in Waterlow Park.

Paul and Diana knew as soon as they saw the house that it was for them. The spectacular views from the rear windows and the attractive, albeit somewhat inaccessible, walled garden, a haven of peace in their busy lives, more than compensated for the intrusion of the traffic. They also found the entrance hall, which had a gallery running around the first floor rooms, very spacious and elegant. The estate agent had no difficulty in concluding a deal at a price which gave little away, and within a matter of weeks the young couple had moved in.

They soon noticed that their cats appreciated the house even more, if that were possible, than they did. They sprawled luxuriously on the landing, on the stairs and in the front hall and reacted as if they were being stroked and caressed by unseen hands. At times they would roll onto their backs and purr loudly as if someone were stroking their tummies, but at other times they would hiss violently at nothing.

"Ghosts of former owners and their dogs." Paul would explain light heartedly to dinner guests and for a time the behaviour of the cats became a regular topic of conversation amongst their friends.

All old houses have their frustrating elements, be they uncontrollable drafts or rampant wood worm, and Rainsborough House was no exception. The single most annoying trait was the jamming of the front door. It happened first a few months after they had moved in and Paul was determined to have it sorted out. A joiner was called to take the door off its hinges, plane the edges down, replace the hinges which were not original but poor Victorian substitutes and rehang the door. For a while this appeared to solve the problem, but one morning, shortly after Paul had left for work, Diana was unable to open the door. Feeling frustrated and worried about missing her appointment, she called Paul on his mobile. Shortly before he returned, Diana tried the door again and without any force being required it opened smoothly on its new hinges.

"It's quite illogical." Diana complained to Paul, feeling both incompetent and angry at the ability of an inanimate object to frustrate the smooth running of her successful career in the City.

Rainsborough House had a further, rather charming, trait which took some months for Diana to notice and which Paul did not entirely believe. If documents, such as files from work or household bills, were casually scattered, maybe the hall table or on the desk in the library, they would often be moved to another place and arranged in almost obsessional order. At first Diana simply believed that she was becoming forgetful, but after some months she became convinced that her papers were being moved. More embarrassing was that on occasions documents were actually taken from her briefcase so that she sometimes arrived at a meeting lacking some crucial evidence. Returning home, she would find the papers neatly stacked in the library. To counteract this, she began leaving her briefcase at work, or locked in the boot of her car. Paul found this very amusing and claimed at dinner parties that his wife's growing absent mindedness could now be explained by the existence of a poltergeist. Diana, who had begun noting where she had left her papers, said nothing in reply.

At first Paul and Diana continued the routine established in their former house of doing housework on a Saturday morning, but as they both progressed up the corporate ladder, they felt they could afford the luxury of a cleaning lady. Some close friends recommended their lady, a strong, sensible and very hardworking Irish lady called Mrs Duffy.

"I can give you two mornings a week, but I must be away by one o'clock as I look after an old lady in the village." She said adding that the house looked remarkably clean, a tribute to the couple's lack of children. Mrs Duffy let herself in after they had both gone to work, cleaned thoroughly and let herself out at one o'clock precisely. The system worked well and the couple rarely met Mrs Duffy, corresponding by notes and leaving the cash on the hall table.

Then one Saturday morning, they were visited by a slightly irate cleaning lady.

"I had the shock of my life last Thursday," she said in a voice which brooked no debate. "I was leaving the house just before one when I found I couldn't open the door. Jammed hard it was, and I felt an awful fool. I phoned my husband to give me a hand, but just before he arrived the door opened. Easy as that. My husband says it must be the weather, as the wood swells in these damp days, but I'm not so sure."

"Not so sure?"

"I'm just not sure at all."

"I'll get the joiner back and we'll have the door sorted out."

"Well, I think I might just stop the job. I've got too much to do."

"Oh please stay, we'll pay some more."

"It's not the pay. It's … it's just that I'm not so sure."

"What do you mean?"

"Well. I've noticed things …"

"What things?"

"Strange little things, like my cleaning things being moved. I could swear that my dusters are moved while I'm cleaning. Pat says I'm doing too much, and he wants me to stop, but as I say, I'm just not too sure. It's a strange house, that's for sure."

They persuaded Mrs Duffy to continue, but the arrangement was not to last. A few weeks later, Diana was called at work by an angry cleaning lady.

"I'm very sorry to phone you at work, but you might have told me about the maid. Gave me a real shock to find her cleaning the bathroom."

"What maid?"

"Your maid. I mean, the house is never really dirty and I can't see the need for me and a maid. Not that I mind, but it gave me the shock of my life."

"We have no maid, what are you talking about."

"Well, it's either a maid I saw or I'm going mad. In any event I'm leaving. There's some houses I like to clean and some I don't, and I just don't like yours."

Diana knew and understood her husband's dislike of the irrational, the inexplicable, and she decided not to mention Mrs Duffy's experience, be it imagined or real. She simply mentioned *en passant* that she was looking for a new daily as Mrs Duffy was finding Rainsborough House too much in addition to her existing commitments.

The real surprise came some months later when Paul had returned home early after an investment trust presentation in a country hotel north of London. Smiling in a slightly conspiratorial way at his wife, Paul said over the dinner table.

"I definitely approve of the new cleaning lady. I don't know if she cleans as well as Mrs Duffy, but she certainly looks much better. I quite fancy the uniform."

"Not the maid," Diana blurted out before having time to consider her response.

"Yes a maid, fully dressed for the part. Young, attractive, hardworking, perfect. Where did you find her?"

Diana made no reply.

"Hey, you're shaking," Paul said putting his arm around her. "What's up?"

"The maid – it doesn't exist. There is no maid. I haven't replaced Mrs Duffy because the house seemed quite clean without her."

"What does that mean – 'There is no maid'? I saw a young girl dressed in a black housemaid's uniform cleaning the stairs outside the bathroom. It's true that she was very shy and said nothing to me, hardly even noticed me, but of course she exists."

"Mrs Duffy saw exactly the same maid and that's why she left. The house is haunted. That's why it was so cheap and that's why nobody stays here for long."

"Rubbish. I didn't study physics at university having come from a totally rational and atheist background, to be told that our house is haunted."

"What about the maid, what about the front door jamming, what about my papers being moved …?"

"I can't believe this, coming from the most rational and coldly logical person I've ever met."

"I know all that, and that's why I've not mentioned my fears to you. But I am really frightened, especially as I'm not sure what's frightening me. Let's take a holiday and come back to a fresh start."

After a spring holiday spent on a quiet Greek island, the couple returned to Rainsborough House and to their jobs in the City, their lives returning to a hardworking but fulfilling routine. Neither mentioned the strange events in the house and the whole subject was banned by mutual and unspoken agreement. However, one night in mid-January, Diana was working late on a complicated case which was to be heard in court the following day. Paul had long since gone to bed, and Diana was working alone in the study, the door to the hall standing open. She was convinced that she had heard a noise in the bathroom, and thinking that it was Paul, she switched off the lights and went up to bed. Paul was asleep in the bedroom, and Diana went along to the bathroom to see if one of the cats was up to its usual trick of climbing up the shower curtain before leaping off. The bathroom door was firmly locked, and she had the impression that she was standing on a wet carpet. Cursing her husband under her breath for his infuriating habit of splashing water over the floor, a common cause of disagreement between them, Diana turned on the hall light. Her stockinged feet were standing in a puddle of fresh blood, which was seeping slowly down the stair carpet.

Too frightened even to scream, Diana ran back to the bedroom to wake Paul. Muttering something about, "Not all this again," Paul put on his dressing gown and crossed the landing to the bathroom, while Diana lay sobbing on the bed.

"There's nothing here," he called out to his wife. "It's another figment of your imagination. You've been working too hard."

"The bathroom door was locked; there was blood under the door. I saw it with my own eyes."

"Nonsense," Paul said as he climbed back into bed. "I thought we had finished with all this."

They talked for a while before Paul put out the lights, but instants later, they both heard a bloodcurdling scream, the scream of a wounded man. Then loud thuds, and the hysterical crying of a woman.

"It's another fight outside The Crown," Paul said reaching out to turn on the lights, but the electricity was cut off.

Going out onto the landing, Paul saw two men, illuminated in ghostly yellow from the street lights, locked in a vicious fight outside the bathroom. As he looked, he saw the younger and stronger man hitting an older man about the head with what looked like a large stone. The older man was putting up a feeble resistance while sliding further and further down the wall, on which a dark blood stain was spreading. Paul rushed forward to intervene but as he did so a slim figure of a girl which he recognised as the maid, ran up the stairs and through Paul, who experienced a shudder of cold horror. Standing aside he watched as the young man and the maid dragged the groaning figure into the bathroom leaving behind a trail of fresh blood. They shut and bolted the bathroom door, but a few moments later the young man reappeared and went down the stairs to return with a heavy bag of tools.

Shaking with terror at the violence of the scene, Paul returned to the bedroom to phone the police, but, as with the lights, the phone was dead. He persuaded Diana, who was hiding in the bed, out onto the landing and down the stairs.

"We must get out and get some help." Paul kept repeating, but as they reached the front door they found it closed and bolted. No amount of pulling would shift the bolts. The windows were also firmly jammed and all attempts to attract the attention of the few passing motorists failed.

"What about the back windows?" Diana cried running across the hall and into the kitchen. "Look, they can be opened!"

Paul restrained her from jumping down 15 feet onto a hard stoned terrace, holding her down on the kitchen floor.

They waited trembling and huddled closely together on the kitchen floor for over an hour. Then they heard the bathroom door opening and saw the young man coming down the stairs with a heavy sack in his hands. Leaving the sack by the front door, he returned to the bathroom for another sack, repeating the operation several times until there was a pile of blood stained sacks by the front door. Then putting his hand into a sack, he pulled out the horrible image of a severed head, still bleeding, its features frozen in a tortured grimace.

"Here's the bastard, your erstwhile lover."

The maid scream hysterically. "Put it away, you murderer!"

The young man then kissed the severed head on its bloody lips. "That's the last kiss you'll enjoy on this earth!"

"Oh God, oh God! How could you!"

"Don't worry about what I'm doing, you get on and scrub the bathroom and stairs. I'll get back to the shop."

He then opened the front door and dragged the sacks outside.

Paul ran over to the door, but it was still firmly jammed. Looking up the stairs, he saw the maid scrubbing the walls and stair carpet. This she continued to do for several hours until the late winter dawn began to break, then coming down the stairs she passed close to Paul and with a little curtsy said, "Just doing my job, sir."

Opening the front door, she went outside, closely followed by Paul and Diana who had finally been released from their torture cell. The maid walked a few yards along Hornsey Lane towards Suicide Bridge before disappearing into the dawn mist.

There was no question of going to work that day, and Diana drove into Hertfordshire to stay with her parents, vowing never to sleep in the house again. Paul's first appointment was with an estate agent before driving to the local library to start research into Rainsborough House. After a few days spent reading scrap books, newspaper cuttings and local histories, Paul was able to piece together the bizarre history of Rainsborough House.

The most concise article appeared in The Hampstead and Highgate Express in January 1938 entitled *Fifty Years Ago – A Triumph of Forensic Science:*

'Fifty years ago this week, the brutal killing of Major Drummond took place in his house on Hornsey Lane, Highgate. The major was a widower who had fallen passionately in love with a maid of 18 years of age who was herself engaged to a local butcher's assistant. The young couple devised a plan whereby she would pretend to be responsive to the major's advances while demanding payments in cash and kind in return. They also hoped to influence the major's will.'

'The plan went wrong when it would appear that the major raped the maid, and in revenge, her fiancé swore to kill him. Together they planned to confine the old man to the house by locking the doors and windows and they hoped that his death by starvation would appear natural. At some stage during the old man's imprisonment, a fight broke out and he was quickly overpowered and murdered. At first his death was not noticed, but after some weeks, neighbours and relatives reported his disappearance to the police.'

'The case was heard in July 1888 and aroused considerable interest. No body was ever found and the defence argued for lack of evidence. However, the jury were persuaded that the defendant, being a butcher and having access to the machinery in his employer's shop, had dismembered the body and probably turned it into dog meat. What finally clinched the case for the prosecution was forensic evidence given by the police who had searched the house meticulously and had discovered traces of blood in the stair carpet. The blood type tallied with his doctor's records enabling the prosecution to claim 'beyond reasonable doubt' that Drummond had been murdered and his body dismembered.'

'The butcher was convicted of murder and hanged after an unsuccessful appeal. As he left the court, there was a dramatic moment when he shouted out to his fiancée, "You killed me. You have my blood on your hands. If you had done your job properly, I would be free. You're the murderer!" The maid was given a surprisingly lenient sentence for the period, the judge possibly sympathising with her predicament. However on her release from prison she committed suicide by jumping off the Hornsey Viaduct, locally known as Suicide Bridge.'

'The judge praised the police for their dedicated and painstaking search of Rainsborough House in particular the work of the forensic scientists, whom he described as "the policemen of the future".'

Paul, who was living with friends, resumed his work later in the week having arranged to meet an estate agent at Rainsborough House on the Saturday morning for detailed measurements to be taken. He was called at work by the agent on Friday afternoon who said that he had taken the measurements of the house, requesting Paul to come to his office on Saturday to discuss price and marketing.

"How did you manage to take the measurements?" Paul asked in some surprise.

"Oh, I was passing the house this morning, and your maid let me in."

# The Perfectionist

## Part One

It would be difficult to find two people more unlike each other: John Skeggs an honest, hardworking teacher who had established a reputation and later a business as a technical wizard and James Houghton, tall, dark, good looking but at heart an actor whose only interest was his own success.

John Skeggs knew the value of money. His father had been a casual labourer, a good brick layer when sober, but a man who drifted between jobs and spend his earnings in the pub. John was brought up in poverty, his mother trying to survive on what little her husband reluctantly granted her and what she could earn serving part-time in a café in South London. With two growing boys to feed and clothe, life was always a struggle. John quickly understood the importance of money and how difficult it was to earn. He did a paper round early in the mornings before going to school, and helped in the Indian corner shop after school. At weekends he often helped out at a local car repair outfit situated under the railway arches in Brixton. By dint of hard work and determination he got a place at Loughborough University to study computing, but was obliged to work evenings and during vacations to make ends meet.

James Houghton's career path could not have been more different. His father was a successful accountant who ran a practice with his wife. James considered them both somewhat boring and risk adverse, but enjoyed a very comfortable life style as a result of their endeavours. He attended a private school in Surrey but suffered from an inherent laziness. Not that he was unsuccessful, far from it, but his success depended on last minute revision, talking his way out of trouble and 'flying by the seat of his pants' rather than hard work and commitment. His teachers despaired, but could not deny that he achieved good exam results and was able to talk his way into a place at university to read history. At Bristol, James was a huge success with his fellow students of both sexes. His brilliant conversation, ability to mimic and see the funny side of any situation, made him both popular and admired. He had a string of girlfriends but his affairs were always short lived. At first impressed by his academic brilliance, his tutors began to suspect that his essays were based on the minimum of reading, the slightest analysis and depended above all upon his command of the written word. They encouraged him to delve deeper into his subject, but in vain.

John left Loughborough with an Upper Second and after a year's DipEd landed himself a job at a grammar school in Buckinghamshire. The job was to teach computing as well as to assist in the IT of the school. He quickly discovered that his IT skills were far superior to anyone within the school and was very quickly in constant demand. Having a very practical mind, he could also help out when lights fused, boilers failed or the headmaster's car would not start. In short he became indispensable which in fact gave him great satisfaction. He was known as a perfectionist because whatever he touched he had to make work smoothly and accurately.

James left Bristol with a poor degree. His tutors had seen through his superficial brilliance and discovered someone unable to grasp original and controversial ideas, and was content to regurgitate accepted theories and interpretations. His departure from the university with a third-class degree went unnoticed, but James' ability to impress on first sight enabled him to find work without a struggle. He had discovered his ability to sell and applied to upmarket car dealerships in central London. He was soon selling Rolls Royces and Bentleys in Barclay Square where his good looks, smart dressing and brilliant sales talk began to earn him good commissions. Eventually however irregularities began to appear in his accounts. He appeared to have given an Italian buyer a substantial discount on a superb new Bentley Continental when a discount of this size was unnecessary to secure the sale. When the management demanded to see James' private bank statement, they discovered a number of payments from their own clients, obviously backhanders for the discounts James had given. Unwilling to draw attention to their own mismanagement, they agreed to dismiss James with a reasonable reference and not take any legal action.

James moved effortlessly from Barclay Square to Bond Street where he got a job selling upmarket jewellery and fashion items. Again his polished manner, excellent dress sense and natural charm endeared him to his customers and he was soon considered a star salesperson by the management. Indeed, when the sales manager, who was unsure about

James's selling techniques, retired, the management appointed James to his place.

It was some years later that James's career again unravelled. A Japanese businessman had bought his wife, for their fiftieth wedding anniversary, a stunning necklace with, at its centre, a substantial and very pure diamond. Sadly, the couple had died some years later and while carrying out the probate, a diamond expert had spotted that the stunning 'diamond' was in fact a fake. Solicitors had contacted James's shop in Bond Street where panic ensued. Someone within the organisation had substituted a fake diamond for the original and had certainly sold the original for a substantial sum. The finger of guilt pointed towards James, but the management were reluctant to call in the police or start a legal affair as the publicity would ruin the business. James protested his innocence but an agreement was reached whereby James left the business with a clean reference. The management feared that other cases of substitution would emerge but hoped that they would be in the very distant future.

For a few years James took various jobs selling high end fashion items, but in fact drifted along supported by the funds he had illegally acquired and with the help of family money. He continued to embezzle when the opportunity arose, but it was not the money that attracted him but rather the excitement of fraud, theft and dishonesty. All this was to change when he met the love of his life – Sandy, a tall elegant red head who swept him off his feet. They met regularly at the best restaurants in the West End, at the most trendy night clubs and jetted abroad for expensive weekends in the sun. After a string of short term affairs, this was the real thing for James and he was determined to marry Sandy. The only problem was the coolness of her parents towards him. Sandy explained that they felt he was a playboy without prospects and wanted him to have a job and some career prospects. James accepted their reservations and agreed to settle down in a solid job.

John Skeggs had become an important figure in his school and rose to become Head of IT. He was unique in having both academic qualifications and a theoretical understanding of computing, while being practical in every way. He was popular with staff and pupils alike and very happy in his job. His personal life changed when he met Sally, a bright, lively girl who joined his computing course in the sixth form. Of course John would never have had a relationship with a pupil, but her very presence seemed to enrich his days. Sally had a broad face with a wide mouth, blue eyes and naturally blond hair. Unlike the other pretty girls in her class, she seemed unaware of her beauty. For two years John admired this girl from a distance and was delighted when she got a place at university to read computer sciences. He was even more delighted when at the end of her first term, she came back to the school to suggest that they might have a meal together in a local restaurant.

Three years later they were married and Sally took a job in a firm selling computer systems to local businesses and advising on updates and improvements. It was a perfect marriage, marred only by their inability to conceive. At first they took medical advice but eventually decided that they might prefer to live without children. Sally was ambitious and often frustrated working in what she considered was a badly run business which missed out on major opportunities. One evening John suggested that she should consider setting up her own company, to which Sally replied that she had been thinking about this for some time. They discussed whether John could be involved in the evenings and at weekends, and whether this would impact on his school career. They eventually decided that Sally would open a business in their joint names and that John might eventually join the business full time if it took off.

The business did flourish, at first with one shop and office in Reading, then a second in Amersham and eventually a third in Slough. John remained at the school for as long as possible, putting in very long hours and working in the evenings and at weekends. Gradually he was forced to cut down his days teaching and eventually decided to devote himself entirely to the business. John was acutely aware of the difference between his childhood poverty and his adult prosperity, but he never lost the value of money. He found it difficult to spend money on luxuries preferring to invest money into their pensions and various saving schemes. They moved into an elegant house in Iver, but John remained constantly aware that it was good fortune and hard work that had brought them prosperity and material comfort.

James had considered where his skills in selling could earn him a good income as well as satisfying Sandy's family, and encouraged by Sandy's father who worked in the City, James enrolled on a one-year course run by the London Institute of Banking and Finance. He applied himself to his studies and at the end of the year passed Unit 1 and Unit 2 which consisted of nine months course work. His intention was to settle into a reasonably well paid job which would allow him and Sandy to continue their expensive lifestyle. After receiving his DipFA, James joined a large City firm of financial and investment managers. Any thought he might have had about working the system to his advantage were quickly dismissed as the company was run with the strictest financial controls in place.

After a sumptuous wedding James and Sandy settled down to an expensive way of life. With a substantial mortgage, they bought a Queen Anne style mansion in Sidcup where they entertained lavishly. They were soon joined by two children accompanied by school fees and other expenses. James enjoyed his job selling investments and giving financial advice, but occasionally wondered whether he could make more money by going 'off piste'. On a family holiday to Spain, they stayed in a hotel which was attached to a golf course. James had always enjoyed a round or two of golf, but it was the chat in the club house that really interested him. He mingled amongst expats who talked about their pensions and shares in what seemed to James a somewhat naïve way, and he decided that his skills could be profitably employed selling investment schemes to British expats in Spain.

In the City, James worked on a self-employed basis and was able to fix his own hours, so the first step was to reduce his City commitments. He then returned to Spain and rented a high street office, with accommodation above, using a new name, Richard Ellis-Jones. He had no difficulty in buying a fake passport under his new alias and as Richard Ellis-Jones he leased a car and enrolled at the golf course he had visited near Malaga. He had the knowledge and experience to talk convincingly about pensions and investments and he had also gathered and copied a huge quantity of paperwork, forms and printed information about the schemes he planned to promote. He fitted out the office with upmarket office furniture and employed an English woman who was bored with her life in

Spain and was looking for something interesting to do. He took out some advertisements in English language newspapers and slowly but surely the punters arrived. For the majority of his clients James provided honest advice, but he kept his eye open for the big fish that would prove to be the real catch.

John and Sally Skeggs had little time for relaxing weekends, let alone holidays abroad, but one evening when John was working late at the office, he suffered an acute and persistent pain in his chest. Sally who was also working late called an ambulance and John was taken to Reading hospital. He had not suffered a heart attack, but his blood pressure was high and the consultant warned him that unless he changed his lifestyle he would likely have a heart attack. This episode changed their lives, as they began to wonder why they worked so hard and why they were so driven. They had no children, no one to leave their money to, no debts and no reason to overwork. A friend suggested that they borrow their villa in Spain for a few weeks to recuperate, and while Sally readily agreed, John was loath to let go of his business even for a few weeks. Sally prevailed and they both enjoyed a relaxing holiday in the sun.

About a year later, the Skeggs received an offer for their business. It was a substantial offer because the business had grown its client base and now employed 15 people in addition to the Skeggs. They sold computer systems, serviced and repaired computers and helped local businesses set up and run bespoke systems. But Sally worried about John, who was unable to stand back or work part-time. Since his health scare they had started taking holidays, but it was obvious that he worried constantly about the business, making innumerable phone calls to check on every minor detail. Here was an opportunity for them both to stop work, enjoy retirement and hopefully better health. So the deal was done, and the Skeggs were freed from their daily routine of hard work.

John found his freedom very difficult to accept and even considered returning to teaching. His belief in hard work was difficult for him to abandon. Sally realised that he needed a new project and suggested they buy a second home in Spain where they had so happily recuperated. They found a late nineteenth century villa in need of restauration but set in wonderful gardens to the South of Malaga and John set about returning the house to its former glory. It was near a golf course and John was soon a regular in the clubhouse. After a couple of years of commuting between Spain and Iver, they decided to settle in Spain and sold the Iver house at a substantial profit.

It was at this point that the lives of John Skeggs and James Houghton would cross with disastrous consequences for both. James was splitting his time between England and Spain, working in the City and living in Sidcup with his family but returning to Spain for a few days every other week. The Spanish business was small and his commissions only just covered his expenses, but he was confident of ensnaring a wealthy client whom he could fleece. Sadly, John and Sally Skeggs were to be his victims. They met at the golf club over drinks at the bar. James quickly sussed that John Skeggs was a very wealthy man, but relatively naïve in financial matters. He obviously had a large amount of cash sitting in the bank but little idea of what to do with it. James realised that he would have to play a slow waiting game. At first he sold John a series of small investment schemes which performed well.

Over a period of two years, he tempted John with more ambitious schemes and in order to establish his credibility, James set up an investment day in the hotel to which he invited his past clients to voucher for his reliability and success.

John and Sally were impressed with Richard Ellis-Jones, as they knew him. He was smartly dressed, played excellent golf, was generous at the club bar, had an office in town and came highly recommended by other club members. They were impressed by the investment day in the hotel and were tempted by James's offer to take full control of a client's finances. John had come to dislike the annoying paperwork that arrived most mornings when he wanted to get on with restoring the house, be out on the golf course, or sailing in his friend's 40 foot ketch. Occasionally he was obliged to return to the UK to meet his bank manager but he found the trips back to the UK increasingly tiresome. After talking things through with Sally, he decided to approach James with the idea of subscribing to his total financial package. James was careful not to show too much enthusiasm at first and played a very cool game, warning John about the dangers of handing over his finances to someone he did not know. John protested that he did know James, had been impressed by the praise heaped on him by his clients and by his deep knowledge of financial affairs. James offered to take the Skeggs out to lunch and asked his assistant to come along to witness the signing of the necessary papers.

At first everything went well for the Skeggs. Their pensions were paid automatically into their Spanish bank account and the return on their investments seemed to increase every month. A few letters continued to arrive at the house, and they forwarded them to James as instructed. James would appear from time to time with papers for them to sign. Every month a detailed account of their investments and bank balance would appear and they both agreed that they were far happier with a professional like James managing their financial affairs.

One day at the club someone mentioned that James's office in town had closed and was up for re-letting. John thought little of it at the time, but about a month later another friend mentioned that James had not been seen in the club for several months. They went to the club secretary to see if there was any news only to be told that Richard Ellis-Jones was no longer a member. John began to wonder what had happened to James and began phoning the London companies whose addresses appeared on the various documents James had provided. To his great concern, no one at any of the companies had heard of a Richard Ellis-Jones. Worse was to follow. That afternoon the manager of their Spanish bank phoned to say that they had overdrawn on their current which had not been agreed. John told him to move money from their various deposit accounts to cover the overdraft, only to be told that all their deposit accounts had been closed and that they had no cash, bonds or any other financial securities to cover their overdraft.

In panic John drove to the bank for a meeting with the manager. His anger was directed towards the manager when he saw his empty accounts, but the manager informed him that he had signed the papers withdrawing the money and the bank had simply followed his instructions. Returning to the house, he phoned his bank in England to find again that the deposit accounts had been closed, but there remained a few thousand pounds in his current account. Going through the large pile of papers that James had sent them on a regular basis he tried to track down his investments only to find that none of the companies held anything in his name. The only income left to the Skeggs was their state pension which James could not touch and a modest teacher's pension. Even their private pensions built up through long years of saving had been emptied. He now had to tell Sally who was happily working in the sunlit garden. Calling her in, he gently went through the dreadful news, trying but failing, to put a brave face on it. All the hard work, their lives with no holidays and few luxuries, their prudence in saving for the future, their fundamental belief that hard work pays – all destroyed by a conman who appeared to have disappeared into the ether. Sally sat immobilised then without saying a word she went up to her bedroom and locked the door.

Over the next few days John attempted to trace the whereabouts of Richard Ellis-Jones. He spoke to his clients at the golf club, only to find that their investments were intact and had actually performed quite well, but none had any current address for Richard. John's next step was to contact the police who showed little interest in the case. They had a record of Richard Ellis-Jones and his address at the shop in town, but nothing more. No complaints had been filed against him. They noted John's case but suggested that it was a matter for the British Police. The ghastly reality slowly dawned that Richard or whoever he was had deliberately set out to defraud the Skeggs and to rob them of everything they had. Their lives had been completely and systematically ruined and it would appear that there was nothing they could do about it.

# Part Two

The last six months of the Skeggs' life in Spain was purgatory for both of them. They had the painful task of selling their house which was beginning to respond to their immaculate restoration, of quitting the golf club and the friends they had made. John spent hours on the phone trying to discover exactly who Richard Ellis-Jones was but made little progress. He had very carefully hidden his trail and even those clients to whom he had sold legitimate policies were unable to discover his real name. Sally had declined into a lethargic pessimism unable to take any interest in life around her. She claimed that she had lost everything and that having sacrificed having a family for the sake of the business she now had nothing to live for. Physically she had aged, her hair had gone white and in places was falling out, and her skin had gone grey.

Eventually the house was sold and the Skeggs moved into a tiny rented house in Surbiton. Built in the 1970s it was a two bedroom house which made up a terrace of equally undistinguished dwellings, its only redemption was having a garage. John contacted an acquaintance who had previously acted as their financial advisor. He listened sympathetically to their story and promised to help, but was unable to locate any person working in financial services under the name of Richard Ellis-Jones. He was also pessimistic about their prospects of recovering the money as they had apparently signed the documents and in a country where the FSCS did not operate. John also had a meeting with the Citizens Advice Bureau, but again with disappointing results. Unless he was prepared to pay for a private investigator and then for a solicitor, little could be achieved and John simply could not contemplate any further expenses. He was also concerned about Sally's deteriorating health. She was experiencing tingling sensations in her limbs and loss of feeling, and was soon diagnosed with Motor Neurone Disease almost certainly brought on by the shock of her loss. John struggled over the next 18 months with an increasingly handicapped wife, before finally losing her battle with MND.

During the last few months of Sally's life, John had abandoned his enquiries and had even stopped opening his mail. Now alone, and indeed lonely, he started picking up the pieces of his investigation. A friend from Spain who had bought an investment scheme from Richard Ellis-Jones had written a letter informing John that by pure chance he had discovered that Richard's real name was James Houghton and that he worked with an investment company in the City. John immediately contacted the company only to find that James Houghton no longer worked there, but at least he had a real name to pursue. Over the coming months he surfed the internet determined to find out more about his nemesis, but it was not easy. He found an address for him in Sidcup, but when he visited the house he was told that the family had left some years earlier with only a post office box as a contact. John came across several references to James Houghton as a financial adviser but in every case he had left the company and they had no knowledge of his whereabouts. It became obvious to John that he no longer worked in financial services.

One evening surfing the net John came across an old article mentioning James Houghton as a member of his school's old boy golf club. He phoned the school the following day to be told that the school never gave out details of former pupil's personal addresses. Feeling that he was getting closer to his prey, John visited the school posing as a grandfather looking to fund a grandchild's place at the school. After a short interview he requested copies of the current school magazine and the old boy's publication. Having established the telephone number of the Hon Sec of the golf club, he phoned and said that he was an old friend of James Houghton, but having lived and worked abroad, he had lost contact with his old golfing partner. The Hon Sec was unable to give out James's address (school policy) but in this exceptional circumstance he was prepared to reveal his telephone number, which luckily for John was a landline and not a mobile.

John now knew that James lived in North London, so the next step was to phone the number pretending to be a delivery company that had been given an illegible address. A man answered the phone saying that he would collect the parcel himself from the delivery company's depot. The following day, John phoned again and this time the phone was answered by a woman, probably a Filipino maid. John told her that he had been asked to deliver a beautiful bouquet of flowers for Mrs Houghton, but did not have the correct address. The maid informed him that they never gave out the address of the house, to which John replied with a touching speech about how sad it would be to see these beautiful flowers wilting and dying before Mrs Houghton could enjoy them. The ploy worked and John now had James Houghton's address, which was in a road in the Hampstead Garden Suburb.

For months even years John had seen the face of the smooth conman who had wrecked his entire life. He dreamt about him, saw his face in crowded places, had visions of meeting him to confront him face to face, and the next step was to visit him at his home. He drove to the road and sat outside the house until he saw James emerging with two small dogs to get into the BMW parked in his drive. For an instant John wanted to rush over and confront him, possibly physically assaulting him. His anger swelled up and he found himself shaking with fury. However, something stopped him, the understanding that he needed to plan his assault carefully to get the maximum satisfaction.

For weeks John considered his options for revenge. He realised that the legal route was barred by costs and lack of evidence. He had been a fool to sign papers without studying them, but that was in the past. What he could achieve now was to frighten him, and the more he thought about it, to kill him. The murder would have to be perfect because John was not prepared to end his life in jail. And yet, it had to be murder because any other form of assault would also see him imprisoned. What weapon would he use? He considered a knife but that would cover him in blood and would not necessarily kill him. If he were also cut during a knife attack, he would leave blood, therefore DNA, at the scene. A gun was a possibility, but he had no access to firearms and if he did obtain one, the police could trace it back to him. He then began to think about a hammer, a simple object which he already had and which could fit into his pocket. He could leave it at the scene of the crime as he would ensure that it had no finger prints. John found an old claw hammer in his tool box and began practicing hitting an object hard with two hands on the hammer. He rigged up a stand which held a melon at what he considered to be James's height and practiced smashing it as hard as he could.

Then he began to consider where the crime would take place. If he attacked James outside his house, he would certainly be seen, and wondered where James was going with his two dogs. He returned several times to the house and noted that at about 11.30 each morning, James set off in his car with the two dogs returning in time for lunch at 1pm. He followed James to Kenwood where he parked in an area beside one of the entrance lodges. From there James walked towards Kenwood House down a path with thick foliage on either side. Provided there were no people about this might be a perfect spot for the attack. John bought an exercise book and began planning the murder in great detail. His overriding concern was to have absolutely no contact with other people and at the same time to check and double check the possibility of being caught on CCTV.

If he drove his own car into Kenwood car park, he would be quickly identified, so he would have to leave his car elsewhere and walk, but this would mean his getaway would be on foot which was dangerously slow. He then decided to use one of the two bicycles that he had in the garage. They were bought years ago and could not be identified. The idea was sound, but the problem was that his current car was small and it was very difficult to get a bicycle into the back. He did not want to be seen struggling with a bicycle in a residential street in North London. He also began to worry that he had driven many times to Hampstead to survey the murder scene and his victim's routine, that the police might pick up his number plate on CCTV. The obvious solution to both problems was to either hire or steal a larger car, probably a big SUV. Hiring involved other people, so he ruled out that option.

Stealing was also dangerous because the police would be on the lookout for the car and he might be stopped either before or after the murder. He then remembered seeing thousands of cars parked at Gatwick airport when he went to the airport on his way to Spain. The official car parks were protected by registration identification and barriers, but there were many hotels and guest houses around Gatwick where people left their cars. The problem was to find one that did not have CCTV. John cruised around the airport noting the names and telephone numbers of hotels and guest houses that offered free car parking. Having bought a cheap mobile phone under a false name, he started calling the hotels requesting information. He soon learnt that most guests arrived on Friday, Saturday or Sunday and left their cars for one or two weeks. The hotel held the keys until their return. Some bigger hotels had barriers and CCTV surveillance, but a few smaller hotels and guest houses did not, stating that they took no responsibility for their guests' cars.

John reckoned that he could steal a SUV from a Gatwick hotel mid-week and return it the following day. The chances of the owners returning mid-week were very small, but how to steal a car without damaging the door while breaking in? John remembered reading an article about thieves targeting certain makes of cars which had keyless entry and using a device bought on the internet were able to clone the card. In theory John would able to identify a large SUV, clone the card, replace the stolen car with his own, drive to within half a mile of his house, load the bicycle into the SUV and set off the following morning to exact his revenge on James

Houghton before returning the SUV to its place in the car park of the hotel at Gatwick. The beauty of this plan being that the owners would have no idea that their car had been stolen, and if the police by chance picked up the registration number, the owners would have proof that their car had been in a car park at Gatwick. The risk was that they would return mid-week but John was prepared to take the risk. He contemplated whether to top up the tank, but decided that it would be safer to keep away from petrol stations which all had CCTV.

John returned to Hampstead a few more times, checking that James Houghton did not vary the time of his morning walk with his dogs. He decided to park the SUV on the Heath Extension and that he would simply abandon the bicycle in the long grass as it could not be traced back to him. The amusing thought passed his mind that he would actually welcome it being stolen! The weather was turning autumnal and John decided that his attack should take place in November when there would be less people around Kenwood, so he planned a time during the school half term when there would be plenty of large cars to steal. John had joined a gym in Surbiton, one of his very few luxuries left to him. He noticed that members presented their entry cards on arrival and the time was logged, but they were not logged out. He decided to start making occasional visits to the gym early in the morning to establish a pattern and he would log in the morning of the murder to establish an alibi should it be required.

The weather forecast for the November half term was perfect – grey skies with some rain. On the Tuesday John drove to Gatwick having identified a number of small hotels and guest houses which fitted his criteria. At first he could find no SUVs but at the fourth venue he saw a large black SUV. Parking his own car, he attempted to clone the entry card and was successful as the SUV's card was hanging in reception near hotel entrance. He moved the SUV and put his car in its place before driving back to a quiet road near his house. He had bought a black track suit, black gym shoes and a black balaclava at a sports shop in Oxford Street, paying cash, and he knew that while he would be caught on CCTV after the murder, it would be virtually impossible to identify him in this black clothing. John also bought a good quality pair of leather driving gloves which would provide the necessary grip on his claw hammer as well as hiding any finger prints. That night he polished the hammer removing any possible finger prints or clues to its origin.

The next morning John woke early, dressed in smart trousers, a blue striped shirt with a red tie over which he pulled the black track suit, cycled to the gym to log in, cycled back to the SUV taking with him a roll of large black plastic refuse bags, loaded the bicycle into the boot and drove to the Heath Extension where he parked. He had worried about the rush hour traffic and the fear of a serious traffic jam, but being half term, the traffic was relatively light and he arrived in good time. He cycled up Ingram Avenue and into Kenwood where he hid himself and the bicycle in the deep foliage overlooking the car park. There he waited until James Houghton arrived to walk his dogs The weather was poor, cloudy with persistent light rain and as a result the car park was nearly empty.

During his wait, John 'psyched himself up' reflecting on the loss of his money, his business, his dear wife and in fact his whole life. His anger grew as he contemplated his reduced circumstances and misery all caused by the greed and viciousness of one man, the man who was now approaching down the path towards him. Just as James passed, John jumped out of the foliage, almost danced towards his victim and with all the strength he could muster, smashed the hammer into his head, quickly jumping back to avoid any blood or flesh in the way he had rehearsed of often in his kitchen in Surbiton. He had imagined that his victim would fall face forward to the ground, but for a second James swung around to look at his assailant. His right eye had been dislodged by the force of the blow and hung on his cheek, his left eye was oozing blood, and his mouth was open in a silent scream. It was a horrendous vision which shocked John to his core. All his calculations had omitted any thought about the actual violence and destruction of the assault. James quickly fell to the ground, his face still staring at John while his dogs began to howl, but because they were on a lead, unable to escape.

Deeply shocked and horrified by his violence, John stood for a moment transfixed by the ghastly image, but within seconds began to follow his plan of action. He dropped the hammer, recovered the bicycle from the foliage, cycled through the car park and down Winnington Road and Ingram Avenue to the parked SUV. He abandoned the bicycle in the long grass, unlocked the car where he stripped off his black track suit and balaclava putting them into several of the black bags. He also removed his shoes, slipping into a pair of loafers he had left in the car. Now looking like a prosperous businessman, he drove back to Gatwick where he replaced the SUV in its original parking space, and loaded his car with the black bags. Driving back to Surbiton in his own car he dumped the tracksuit, balaclava and shoes in different locations. He arrived back at his house shocked but also elated. His plan had worked precisely and he now had to tie up a few loose ends. He burnt the exercise book in which he had so painstakingly planned the attack and destroyed the mobile phone he had used. He then sat back and awaited developments.

The murder was reported nationally and on Saturday John took the Underground up to Hampstead to buy the local newspaper which carried a long article about the murder. He learnt that despite appeals to the public, very few people had come forward. No one had witnessed the murder, although a few people had seen a man in black on a bicycle, which was soon found by the police. It bore no clues, no blood or samples for DNA analysis. He also read that the police thought that the murder was probably a professional hit job. Apparently James Houghton was involved in illegal trades in diamonds, selling artificial diamonds to unsuspecting clients and the police thought that he had maybe angered powerful dealers or cartels. One commentator suggested that the police would probably never find the killer.

For a while John basked in his success. Despite having lost everything with no possibility of recovering his wealth and happiness, he felt satisfaction that he had personally avenged himself on his nemesis. He took a part time job working in a big hardware chain of shops where his experience and knowledge made him a respected member of staff. He began to make a few friends amongst the older staff and was even asked to join them at the local pub. He had the state pension plus his teacher's pension to live on, and his new job provided a little extra. Life did not seem too bad, and certainly much better than the last few years.

The problems began when John started having visions. The vision was always the same – that terrible face of James Houghton with its eye hanging down the cheek and its mouth open in a horrendous silent scream – but it appeared in different places and circumstances. At first he saw it in his dreams and he would awake drenched in sweat, but then it appeared in public places. He was working out on a treadmill in the gym and turned to greet the man who had taken the machine next to him, when he saw that it was a vision of James covered in blood, his face staring at John. Terrified John jumped off the machine and ran out into the foyer still in his gym clothes. More concerning was that the vision began to appear at his work place. He was mixing paint for a customer when looking up, he saw that the customer had been transformed into the ghastly vision of the dying James Houghton. The same happened a few days later when John was advising on door hinges, but this time he stood back shouting at the vision to go away. Customers began to complain about his eccentric behaviour and eventually he received a written warning. But the worst visions still came at night. He would see Sally standing at the end of his bed embracing James and covered in his blood. Waking up he would shout at the vision which slowly faded into the darkness. John had such disrupted sleep that he came to fear the nights, often walking the streets to avoid sleep or watching television late into the night. But the vision followed him, ambushing him in the streets of Surbiton or appearing on television while he was fully awake.

Lacking sleep, terrified and haunted by his visions, John began to turn into a physical wreck. He lost his job which was also his lifeline and lived like a hermit in constant fear of his ghosts. Finally, he came to the conclusion that the only possible redemption would be to admit his crime and suffer the legal penalty which might at least exorcise his ghost. He went into the local police station to confess his crime. He was taken into an interview room where he described the murder in detail which was recorded and typed out to be signed. This John did before asking whether he would be detained. The young detective constable asked him to wait and promised that she would return soon. Sometime later she returned and told him he was free to go.

A week later John returned to the police station to be told that the police were not convinced by his evidence and still believed that the murder had been a professional hit job. John protested, arguing that he had provided the details of the murder to which the police replied that he could have read this in the press and above all he had absolutely no evidence of his involvement. The harder he protested, the more the police considered him an eccentric, one of many who claim to have committed a murder in order to gain publicity. He was finally given a warning that unless he left he might be prosecuted for wasting police time.

John returned to his tormented life, rarely sleeping, living in constant fear of James Houghton. Eventually he decided to join his wife Sally as the only way out. As ever he planned his death precisely, cementing a hook into the garage ceiling, buying a length of rope, carefully placing a step ladder which he could kick away. Sadly, he tied the noose badly, and having kicked away the step ladder was left to suffocate in agony over 20 minutes when the slip knot failed to tighten. For the first time in his life, and indeed the last, his perfectionism had failed him.

Milton Keynes UK
Ingram Content Group UK Ltd.
UKHW020736191123
2823UK00012BA/266